To Terri –
I hope you enjoy meeting Josephine –
she exists within every woman.
Fond regards –
Christine

C. A. DANO

Cover Photo: Dennis Rovnak
Cover design: Jay Cookingham
Interior design: Jay Cookingham

ISBN: 1-58776-830-5

Library of Congress catalog card number: 2005923159

Manufactured in the United States of America

0 1 2 3 4 5 6 7 8 9 10 NetPub 0 9 8 7 6 5

675 Dutchess Turnpike, Poughkeepsie, NY 12603
www.hudsonhousepub.com (800) 724-1100

To Pat—
*who convinced me I could . . .*

To Ann—
*who allowed me to color outside of the box . . .*

And to Michael—
*for the gift of time.*

*For Kaitlyn*

ᏍᏓ

*Life is not measured by the number of breaths we take,*

*but by the moments that take our breath away.*

*Anonymous*

☙

ൽ

# Prologue

1984

Nothing as devastating or embarrassing as this had ever happened to her. Even now, with the divorce papers signed, Josephine couldn't believe either she or her husband, now an ex-husband, had actually gone through with it. What was more unbelievable was how she had simply given up and given in, accepting Anthony's false accusation of irreconcilable differences and ultimately agreeing to sign the papers that legally ended their seven-year marriage.

After trying for two years to conceive, Josephine had found out that she was unable to bear a child. Anthony was adamant about fathering his own to ensure the family lineage. As ludicrous an excuse for divorce as it was, one only needed to know Anthony and his archaic Italian family to understand the validity in their demand that the marriage be terminated. It seemed to matter little that Anthony and Josephine had been high school sweethearts. What began as a teenage romance and graduated to marriage, albeit an elopement, had now deteriorated to the point where neither love, nor civility, remained.

Josephine reflected as she sat in a chair with her calico cat, Sundae, curled contentedly in her lap. Sitting there, she had a surreal feeling, almost as if she was floating outside her own body. With her marriage to Anthony now legally dissolved and their house soon to be sold, the prospect of an uncertain future loomed large. Her mother had died when Josephine was a child, and her father had moved across country and remarried while she was still in college. She therefore had no parental influence to help her with these vicissitudes, only a younger married sister with a family of her own.

She hadn't eaten breakfast, and it was nearing noon. A rumbling in her stomach reminded her she should make herself some lunch, but she'd settle instead for a quicker fix: a third cup of coffee. Lifting Sundae from a cozy slumber, she dropped the cat to the floor and went to the kitchen with her coffee mug in hand. She noticed the morning paper on top of the countertop, its front-page cover story on the new owners of a well-established flower shop in Clapton, an hour's drive away. As Josephine scanned the article, she saw mention that the owners were advertising for a window designer and wondered how, with an art degree from Parsons which would over-qualify her for the job, she could possibly support herself. Still, the thought of working in such serene surroundings as a flower shop was appealing.

She had no sooner poured her coffee and settled back in her chair, when Sundae sprang from floor to lap. Josephine reached down to stroke her furry head, and Sundae snuggled closer against the pressure. The cat's golden eyes began to close until they became mere slits as she relaxed to the rhythmic petting.

Within minutes, Josephine's own head had sagged to one side, as she joined her pet in a momentary cat nap while contemplating answering the ad. If she landed the job, it would mean leaving her current position as a graphic artist and moving from all that was familiar. But she was young and strong and anxious to put some miles between her and Anthony. More than that, she was ready for a major life change.

# One

1999

ᏣᏒ

ᘓ

# CHAPTER *One*

The owners of the *Pocketful of Posies Flower Shop* prided themselves on the fact that their customers could be assured of purchasing a memorable statement at a fair price—a reputation which had, from early on, helped draw clientele from all over New England.

It was located on the northeast corners of Main Street and Jefferson and was the most popular store in the town of Clapton, Massachusetts.

Its ivory clapboard storefront and tall windows boasted an oval stained glass window of scarlet peonies above two French doors which served as its entryway. These were wide enough to open when good weather prevailed, and on those days passersby could easily step in to view the wonderland of nature awaiting them inside.

Customers were beckoned to enter, drawn by exotic fragrances and country-type buckets filled with flowers of every possible variety, clay statues, hand-crafted pottery, and contemporary wooden carvings.

Marsha and Marc Silverman, horticulturists with degrees from Cornell University, had moved to Clapton fifteen years ago, when they bought a home on the outskirts of town, purchased the flower shop, and rented the apartment above it to Josephine Mitchell.

At five o'clock, on a Friday evening in April, Josephine pulled the drawer from the register, marking the end of her work day.

"I won't be sorry to see this day end, she said," stepping over Minna, the Silvermans' black Labrador retriever, who lay sleeping in the middle of the wooden floor of the flower shop.

Handing the drawer to her employer, Josephine frowned. "The Hamiltons certainly spared no expense for their daughter's wedding. Just look at my hands!"

She leaned against the countertop, hanging her fingers like a bunch of bananas on display. Several runaway strands of hair had managed to escape the bonds of her French braid and clung damply around a flushed face that had recently begun showing signs of middle age.

"Don't you go blaming those calluses on me; I warned you this wedding would be a killer." Marsha Silverman, a boss in every sense of the word, had a personality as fiery as her red hair. She was only a year older than Josephine, but together they shared a mutual respect as well as a cherished fifteen-year friendship. "And so, tell me why after all these years you need reminding to wear your gloves when you're working?" Marsha stood with arms akimbo and peered over the rims of her bifocals.

"I wore gloves...most of the time. These hands are the result of one who is over-worked and underpaid." A small w formed between Josephine's arched brows. "It's a wonder I have any feeling left in my fingers!"

"I'll bet Ned wore *his* gloves," Marsha chided.

"He doesn't need gloves, he's a guy!"

"A fact some might argue." Marsha put the drawer in the safe, closed the heavy door and spun the combination lock. "Tell you what. You agree to have dinner with Marc and me tomorrow night, and I'll treat you to a manicure after we finish setting up for the wedding."

"Again you're pushing this dinner thing. How many times must I tell you I don't accept blind dates? Why won't you listen to me?"

"Liam O'Dell is not *blind*," Marsha joked, "he's a doctor!"

"A doctor who lives nearly four hours away, now that's tempting."

"Come on, be a sport. Besides, he's Marc's neighborhood crony from a thousand years ago. I don't want to have to entertain him by myself."

"You won't have to. Marc will be there. If you run out of things to say, you can always *wow* him with accounts of your gall bladder attacks." Josephine's brown eyes now danced with humor.

"Liam O'Dell wouldn't be interested in my gall bladder. He's a gynecologist," Marsha said, "and an Irish gentleman. So what's wrong with that? You're allergic, or something?"

"Not at all," Josephine mused. "I wear green on St. Patrick's Day, and once I cooked a corned beef, but it turned out a little tough." Her teasing fell on deaf ears.

"It hurts me to see you alone every weekend because any guy you meet is never your *type*, whatever that is! You need to get back to the land of the living."

"I'm living."

"If you can call being celibate *living*," Marsha muttered. "I'll bet you and Liam would find you have a lot in common if you would give him a chance. You're both single, decent looking, and interesting people to talk to. And I can't speak for Liam, but you, my dear, are long overdue for a fling. Why not join us tomorrow night? You might just like this guy."

"Oh, sure, just what I need—a gynecologist. That's romantic. And unless he hates your gefilte fish recipe, we don't have *zilch* in common. And who says I've been celibate? Did it ever occur to you that maybe, just maybe, you don't know everything about me?"

"But I do know everything about you because you always tell me everything," Marsha said.

"I've dated, I just haven't found the right one yet," Josephine said glumly. "Despite his faults, Anthony was special in a lot of ways."

"Anthony was a jerk." Marsha mumbled.

"What?"

"Nothing. Come on, sweetie. Please? Don't leave me with a roast chicken and two middle-aged roomies drinking beers and telling lies! I promised Marc I'd find Liam a dinner date." Marsha's hand flew up to her mouth. "Oops! Sorry. Did I use the word *date*? I meant to say we need a fourth person to even out the table." Her persuasive smile was hard to resist. "Look, if it feels too much like a fix up, I'll invite Ned and Matthew, too. So, I'll roast another chicken. What do you say?" She clasped her hands in mock prayer.

"I don't know..."

"If you don't come, I may have to think seriously about firing you."

"*You* pay unemployment? I doubt it! But my refrigerator is empty, and I do love your cooking. Okay, I'll come. But only on two conditions."

"Name it, you got it."

"Number one, no gefilte fish..."

"I always thought you loved my gefilte fish."

Josephine raised an eyebrow.

"Okay, okay," Marsha agreed. "What else?"

Josephine held up her hands. "Number two, I'm taking you up on that manicure."

She parked her white Honda Accord beside a shiny black Mercedes convertible with the license plate *DRDAD*. Marsha had failed to mention that Dr. O'Dell was a father. Josephine reached for her lipstick to reapply it before getting out of her car but thought better of it. No sense in looking like I'm interested in the guy, she thought. Instead she gave herself a fleeting once-over before opening the car door and stepping out onto the large circular drive. Landscaped gardens framed a white stucco house. The evening was exceptionally seasonal; the sky turning a shade of blue heather in preparation for the starry night ahead.

She lifted the mass of tousled blond hair from her shoulders, fluffed it and let it fall back into place as she rearranged the light wool shawl over her shoulders. Beneath it she wore a simple black jersey dress.

She prayed her anxiety did not show as she walked up the curved sidewalk and rang the doorbell. Her last thought before Marc Silverman opened the front door was that she had always wanted a child.

"M-m-m, something smells delicious! What did you tell me you're making for dinner?" Josephine placed a homemade apple cake on the center aisle and accepted a glass of chilled white wine from Marc, all the while her eyes scanning the perimeter for the mystery guest.

"As if you care," Marsha replied. "My mother's chicken recipe, remember?" She dried her hands on the chef's apron she wore over a pair of red slacks and a white cashmere sweater. With a flick of her wrist she dropped a morsel to the floor where Minna sat waiting. Like an alligator biding its time, the dog caught the tidbit and, in an instant, gobbled it whole and stood ready for more. "Now if I were the true Jewish princess Marc is always claiming I am," Marsha teased, "I'd have made *reservations* for dinner."

"You are a Jewish princess, and you make plenty of reservations as far as my wallet is concerned. It's about time we had a home-cooked meal." Marc, a small balding man who always looked burdened with the worries of the world, circled his wife's waist with one arm and gave it a playful squeeze as he refilled her glass of wine. "Ned and Matt are with the Doc. They took him outside to peruse our gardens. They'll be in any minute," he said. "Let's *nosh* while we wait." He slapped together a miniature sandwich of crackers and smoked salmon, popping it into his mouth with gusto. Then he spread a spoonful of liver pâté on a sliver of dry toast and fed it to his wife, who accepted the offering and groaned with delight.

Josephine fought the urge to peek out the window, deciding instead to pick from the platter of hors d'oeuvres.

"The shrimp are outrageous! I'm dead and in heaven," she swooned, as she opened her mouth wide to plop a saucy fish inside. No sooner had she done it, then she was sorry. The shrimp was too large, and the cocktail sauce squirted unattractively out of both sides of her mouth. She was trying her best to swallow when a hand gripped her shoulder, catching her off guard. The wine in her glass sloshed over her hand and on to the floor as Josephine hurried to swallow the partially chewed shrimp.

"Sweetie, just look at you all dolled up! Why, you look simply divine!" It was obvious by the elevation in his voice that Ned had been into the wine for some time already. "Doesn't our girl look ravishing, Matthew?" he asked, addressing his partner. Then he turned. "Doctor Liam, this is Josephine Mitchell, my partner in crime at the shop."

Josephine quickly dabbed her lips with the cocktail napkin she held in her hand.

"Ms. Mitchell, my pleasure." Liam O'Dell extended a hand, managing to suppress a smile. Josephine's comical awkwardness had captivated him. He looked at her mouth and thought about letting her know she had missed a spot of sauce, but thought better of it.

"It's nice to meet you." Josephine smiled weakly at the doctor, surprised at how attractive she found him to be, and all the while unaware of the red glob beneath her lower lip.

As Liam excused himself to help Marc retrieve some serving dishes from a cabinet, Ned came forward to wipe the remains of cocktail sauce from Josephine's face with the tip of his little finger. He planted a kiss on her cheek before joining Marsha at the stove.

Left alone, Josephine was free to take a mental inventory of Liam O'Dell, MD.

She guessed him to be about six-foot-two, with an expanse of shoulders that stretched beneath the light blue oxford shirt he wore with the sleeves rolled up. He stood with his feet apart and his hands relaxed in the pockets of a pair of gray wool slacks. Josephine took a sip of wine, tilting her head to one side while she silently admired the fabric of those slacks, which fit as if they had been made especially for him.

His skin was mildly weathered, but soft enough to hold a close shave at this late hour; while his hair, dense and turning prematurely gray, was cut short and neatly combed back from his face.

Liam turned to speak in low tones to those around him, and Josephine noticed a noble brow, which accentuated a pair of ardent green eyes. A shiver ran through her as she envisioned the doctor's patients lying nearly naked on his examining table under the scrutiny of those eyes.

She took into account Liam's misshapen nose, which was slightly larger than it should be, and the boyish curve of his lips. He was by no means perfect, but on a scale of one to ten, Dr. Liam O'Dell was an eleven.

Sauces were stirred, salads were tossed, and foods were transferred from the oven to the top of the stove. Just as Ned's shrill voice had reached an irritating pitch, a perspiring hostess breathlessly announced, "Dinner is served!"

The evening's seating had been purposely arranged to alternate the three couples. Matthew was seated beside Josephine, and Liam on the opposite side of the table next to Ned. Marsha and Marc took their rightful places at either end.

Liam lifted his glass to offer a toast of thanks, only to be rudely interrupted by Ned, who was well on his way to being intoxicated.

Marsha reclaimed the verbal ball by asking Liam to talk about his profession. He gave a somewhat dry account of his obstetrics practice, explaining that he had come to stay with Marc and Marsha on his return from a medical conference in Boston. He mentioned that his home was in the town of Waterbridge and was relieved that no one at the table, other than Marsha and Marc, knew it to be one of the wealthiest suburban towns in the state of New York.

Liam assured them that while his practice provided a lucrative clientele, it also was an occupation that put unavoidable restraints on his personal life. Josephine asked if this didn't bother him.

"Yes, of course it does." He shifted slightly in his seat. "And I plan to correct that," he said. He then spoke of his fourteen-year-old daughter, Meeghan, who had been born in Ireland while he was completing his residency. He looked directly at Josephine when he said this, watching to see if she would be repelled by the thought of his having a child. But she only smiled, and the warm reassurance of it helped him to visibly relax.

"It's too bad your daughter couldn't come with you," she said. "We would have enjoyed meeting the person who inspired your license plate."

Dinner began with crisp salad greens served with mandarin oranges and walnuts and seasoned with a delicate citrus dressing. The chickens, arranged on a platter, were accompanied by a serving bowl of baked scalloped potatoes, encrusted with cheddar cheese and another of fresh asparagus and baby carrots. A basket containing thick slices of warm challah bread and sweet butter was passed around the table.

The wine flowed while conversations at the table ranged from politics to the financial state of the country to religion.

"Our parents' childrearing was clearly unusual for the times," Liam said. "They encouraged us to share in the traditions of each other's religion. I'd sometimes go to temple with Marc, or he would come to my church with me."

Marc agreed. "Between the priest saying the mass in Latin, and our rabbi singing service in Hebrew, I'm surprised Liam and I didn't both become agnostics."

"My grandparents were orthodox Jews," Marsha said. "They wouldn't come to our wedding because the hall we rented in Manhattan wasn't kosher." She turned to Liam and queried, "Which reminds me, are you into gefilte fish?"

"I am so *not* into family!" Matthew said, still on the subject of relatives. "I'm glad Ned and I didn't have to go through any hassles with meddling in-laws." He reached over to stroke his partner's back. "I'm all for cohabitation without representation."

"What about you, Josie?" Ned asked. "Would you ever cohabit?"

"I already do...with Sundae." She looked at Liam and explained, "She's my cat."

"Ned, do not believe for one minute that you are sober, or smart enough to bait Josephine," Marsha warned. "She's on to your tricks. Make yourself useful and help me bring these plates inside, will you?" Marc and Matthew also rose to help, insisting Liam and Josephine remain seated.

The doctor cleared his throat. "Marsha tells me you are an extremely talented designer. I believe she referred to you as 'the heartbeat' of their store."

"Oh, I wouldn't say that. Perhaps she meant the *headache*."

"So you're modest *and* beautiful. I'd like to see your work sometime."

"Sure. Whenever. I'm always there unless, of course, I happen to be upstairs. I live above the shop. It's just Sundae and me...cohabiting." She heard her broken speech, and felt tongue-tied.

Liam grinned. "So you said."

Marsha brought the dessert to the table. She had baked her popular pound cake made with ground walnuts, cinnamon and chocolate chips. On another plate was Josephine's apple cake. Both were served with coffee and a round of after dinner cordials.

It was nearing midnight when the guests took their cues from Marsha, whose mascara had begun to smudge beneath her eyes.

Liam, who wasn't leaving until the next day, offered to walk Josephine out to her car. She kissed Marc, who gave her a secretive wink behind Liam's back. Josephine dismissed it with a haughty look and, with a last farewell to Marsha and the men, stepped out into the brisk night air.

Her heels clicking on the sidewalk was the only sound heard as she and Liam walked in silence across the dimly lit driveway. She knew he was looking at her from behind, and the thought did not displease her. When they reached her car, Liam opened the door for her. Unfolding her shawl, he leaned in close and wrapped it gently around her shoulders. He let his warm hands rest there for just a moment. Josephine's eyes were level with his neck. She noticed his heartbeat pulsing beneath the hollow in his throat. There was a clean, citrus smell about him—a mix of leather and oranges—which she would recall long after they had said goodnight.

Liam took hold of her hand. "It was a pleasure to meet you, and I meant what I said before. I'd like to see you again some time... very soon."

ଓ

# CHAPTER *Two*

The slate blue sky with its low-setting sun marked the end of another work day. The sidewalks were nearly empty of shoppers; Clapton was closing down for the evening.

The man seated on a wrought iron bench across the street from *Pocketful of Posies* was in no rush. Not only was he relaxed, but by the look on his face, he was obviously enjoying his view. He sat to one side of the bench with his arms folded across his chest, his left ankle resting on his right knee as he amused himself with the goings on in the window across the street.

Inside the shop, Josephine was bent over, her derrière shifting from side to side as she rearranged and reconstructed her design for the month of May, the theme of which was *Country Wedding Bouquets.* The window was climate-controlled to aid in the preservation of the flowers and plants on display. This particular assembly called for two mannequins, in full wedding regalia, rented from a Boston bridal shop.

The motionless porcelain bride was wearing a simple sleeveless gown of white peau de soie. On its head was a headpiece reminiscent of a woman's English riding derby with a gathering of tulle, which hung crisply off the rim of the hat and gathered in the back.

The hands of the mannequin bride had been positioned just below the waist. There Josephine attached a small cascading bouquet of twenty champagne roses along with stems of white stephanotis whose stark-white petals stood out prettily against the tendrils of delicate English ivy.

The mannequin's maid of honor wore a soft periwinkle blue gown. She stood staring doe-eyed at the bride, carrying in her posed hands a circular bouquet of yellow roses with tiny blue forget-me-nots dotted throughout. At the hem of her gown were another two coordinating bouquets, suggesting the unseen bridesmaids.

On one wall inside the window hung a noble equestrian print on loan from a local patron's estate. Below it Josephine had placed an antique side table with a silver tray displaying several small boutonnières meant for the imaginary groom and his ushers.

She stood up, and with her hands on the small of her back, bent backward to stretch her spine. Rubbing her hands on her jeans and pushing her hair back from her face, she surveyed her creation.

The man on the bench watched as she stepped down from the window and disappeared. He rose from his seat and crossed the street just as Josephine was flipping the sign on the door to read *Closed.* She was turning the key in the lock when he came up behind her, taking her by surprise.

"Forgive me, I didn't mean to frighten you." Liam O'Dell's face was before her. "It seems I have a knack for catching you off guard."

"It seems that you do!" Josephine exclaimed, recalling the cocktail sauce moment. "What are you doing here?" She wished she was wearing lipstick and had a breath mint in her mouth.

The doctor looked fresh and clean in khaki slacks and madras shirt and a light windbreaker draped over his arm.

"I played in a golf tournament this morning in Westchester. It was a fund-raiser for our hospital. Seeing as it was over by noon, I thought it was a nice day for a ride."

"All the way to Clapton?"

"Sure, why not?"

"It's a four hour drive from New York!"

"I didn't like what they were serving for lunch," he grinned. "I thought I might have better luck with dinner. May I talk you into joining me?"

Josephine was elated. "If you can give me ten minutes to freshen up, you're on. But I'm warning you, I haven't eaten all day. I'm going to be an expensive date."

Liam followed her around the back of the building to a door that opened to a stairwell. At the top, she unlocked another door, and they entered her apartment. At this hour the interior appeared gloomy until the two living room lamps were lit, transforming the color of the walls to a soft creamy yellow. The tall double-hung windows were draped to their sills in a tasteful country print, and the hardwood floors were highly polished with oriental rugs laid over them. The furniture looked inviting.

"Please, make yourself comfortable and have a look around," she said, giving the room the once-over and hoping she had left it presentable. She headed for the kitchen in search of the cat, though she knew from experience that Sundae was hiding from the houseguest. "Can I offer you a drink? Some wine perhaps?"

"No thanks." Liam stood in the doorway watching her open a can of cat food.

Josephine wrinkled her nose at the smell of it, portioned it into a small bowl, washed the fork in the sink, and pulled a paper towel from the roll to dry her hands. "Keep your eye out for my cat. I'll just be a minute," she said, excusing herself from the kitchen. Liam only slightly moved as she passed through the doorway on the way to her bedroom. Their bodies brushed, and the contact set Josephine's heart racing.

Liam made his way around the living room. He walked around with his hands in his pockets, appreciating Josephine's taste, her sense of style and tradition. He approved of her choices in art work: a few simple seascapes and some still-life prints.

His eyes were drawn to a print by Charles Wysocki, hanging in the dining room. It was a painting of a woman standing at the top of a long flight of stairs. She was staring out a window, and in her hand she held an opened letter; its envelope lay on one of the bottom steps.

"It's entitled *Another Year At Sea.* It's my favorite painting...from his lighthouse series." Josephine stood beside him, freshly dressed in a pair of pale blue slacks and a soft yellow sweater. She wore small gold seashell earrings. She smelled of lavender.

"This is an interesting piece," Liam commented.

"Yes, for me there's something mystical about it. Did you know that there's an American flag in almost every painting by Wysocki?"

"Well he must have left it out of this one." Liam stretched his face closer to examine.

"No, it's there. Keep looking."

"I give up."

"Right *there*," she said, pointing to the print where a minute flag stamp was intricately painted on an envelope.

"No wonder I couldn't see it."

Sundae suddenly surfaced from behind the sofa. She bypassed the tall stranger to dart behind Josephine's legs.

"There you are, my darling! Come meet Doctor O'Dell." Josephine stooped to scoop up the oversized calico, who regarded the visitor with skepticism.

Liam reached out to pet her, but the cat crouched down inside its owner's hands, like a turtle retreating into its shell.

"Perhaps some other time," Josephine said, bending to drop her pet to the floor. Sundae looked back for a moment before scampering off to the kitchen.

"Tell me about these pictures," Liam asked, crossing the room. "They must be your family; I can see the resemblance."

They stood together beside a drop-leaf mahogany table where several family photos were displayed. The pride in Josephine's eyes as she identified her relatives intrigued Liam, as well as her description of them, which left him with a longing for family ties.

"And this is my younger sister, Alexandra. We call her Alex. This is her husband, Robert, and my five year old nephew, Robby. They live on Cape Cod. Robert's a fisherman there, and Alex is an interior decorator."

The woman in the photograph had the same eyes as Josephine, but she was taller and had dark hair. The boy could have passed for Josephine's son.

"Your nephew looks a lot like you," Liam noted.

"Yes, he does. He calls me 'Auntie Josie.' I love the way he says my name."

"So, *Josie*," Liam mimicked, "I'm getting hungry, and I know you already are. What do you say you show me how talented the chefs are in Clapton?"

It was a short walk to *The Poseidon Adventure*, a dimly-lit restaurant where no one left hungry and the food was notoriously delicious. After sharing an order of fried calamari and a Caesar salad for two, they ordered entrees of grilled salmon and mesquite swordfish.

Their conversation led to talk about the practice and how Liam managed coverage while being away from the office. He spoke of Ira Goldstein, a promising young intern, who had graduated at the top of his class and whom he would one day consider inviting to join him as a partner in the practice.

Liam asked Josephine about her schooling and how she came to choose her profession. While they sipped creamy cappuccinos, he asked if she minded being so closely connected to her employers, as both employee and tenant. He was not surprised to hear her say that she considered the Silvermans more friends than bosses and that they had always respected her privacy.

After dinner they strolled back toward Josephine's apartment in the peacefulness of night, guided by the pale moon and an occasional street lamp under which tiny insects darted within the haloes of light.

Liam reached down with an open hand to enfold Josephine's small one. It felt comfortable for them both. She looked up at the scattering of stars and sighed dreamily. "Tomorrow should be a beautiful day."

Liam's mind was not on the forecast. "Josie, I was told you aren't seeing anyone...seriously, I mean."

Josephine's eyes were downcast, but the moon illuminated her face enough for Liam to notice the way her feathery lashes cast shadows upon her cheeks.

"That's true."

"That's good news because I would like very much to start seeing you...seriously, I mean."

Josephine couldn't help but smile at his tender approach. "I'm afraid I haven't dated very much since my divorce."

"I don't understand why not," Liam said, perplexed by the fact that this beautiful woman hadn't remarried by now.

Josephine inhaled deeply of the fresh night air before letting it out with a sigh. "Anthony left me when I couldn't become pregnant."

Liam flinched. "And for that he divorced you?"

"He came from a very old-fashioned Italian family. They were adamant about carrying on the family name." She could see by his expression that Liam was amazed at such reasoning.

"After the divorce," Josephine continued, "Anthony went back to further his education, and I went back to my maiden name."

The doctor in Liam could not resist asking. "I gather you both underwent tests?"

"Yes, of course. We discovered that the problem was with me. Endometriosis. Anthony refused to consider adoption. His lack of support was difficult enough, but his leaving did an emotional number on me. I never wanted to go through that again...explaining my condition and all."

"I can understand."

Josephine tossed her head as if to shake off the painful memory, her moonlit hair swaying with the motion. "What about you? Are you seeing anyone?" They had arrived at the door to her apartment.

Liam paused, carefully choosing his words. "There's a nurse at our hospital. We had been seeing each other on occasion." He watched her visibly stiffen before her shoulders slumped. He took her two hands and held them in his own. "It's not serious between us, at least not on my part."

"What about on her part?"

"The only part I want to think about is whatever part includes *you.* I'd like to see you again—often. I don't mind making the drive here, and I'm hoping that you will come to my place. We're close to Manhattan, and there is so much to do there." He reached for a deeper meaning. "Most of all I'd like very much for you to meet Meeghan. I believe you would like each other." He paused. "You know, Josie, we're not kids anymore, either of us. I wouldn't put any pressure on you; I've already got a child." He sucked his lip in contemplation. "What I am trying to say is that I want a future with someone who could love me and, hopefully, my daughter. There, I've said it."

"What about your nurse?" Josephine asked. Her decision depended on his answer.

"She's not *my* nurse, she's just *a* nurse. I never saw myself falling in love with her."

"Does this nurse have a name? We're talking about her as if she doesn't exist."

"Her name is Michelle. And she doesn't exist —at least not for me, anyway, not anymore."

It seemed an eternity before she finally spoke. "I'll look forward to meeting your daughter."

Liam's hands encircled her waist, pulling her closer to him. It was a gentle kiss, a lasting one. Josephine laid her head against his chest and listened to the rhythmic beating of his heart. The sound soothed her, as did the warmth of him. Time seemed to stand still while they stood there together reveling in the moment. The night crickets chirped shrilly.

Above them, in the dimly lit bedroom of the apartment, Sundae lay curled upon the sill. She sat as motionless as a statue, watching the couple below with narrowed yellow eyes. Only her tail moved as it nervously twitched from side to side. Fiercely protective of her mistress, the cat seemed to sense the kiss happening. Silently she jumped down to the floor and, in a matter of seconds, was sitting erect behind the kitchen door like an irate parent whose child has defied her curfew.

# CHAPTER *Three*

"At twenty weeks, your baby is about a foot long and weighs one pound," the doctor said, while slowly gliding the transducer in short circles over the patient's lubricated abdomen.

This was the couple's first baby, and the sonogram reading was thrilling for them, both husband and wife looking like children themselves as they watched the picture moving across the monitor screen with wide-eyed fascination.

"Your baby is already beginning to grow hair, and it has eyebrows and eyelashes," the doctor continued. He was careful with the transducer not to reveal the gender of the fetus to parents who wanted the element of surprise at the delivery of their firstborn.

This was Liam's last patient for the day, and he was anxious to finish the appointment and go home. When the sonogram was finished, the nurse handed the couple the photographic printout and helped ease the pregnant woman to a sitting position.

"Finish getting dressed, Elizabeth, and then you and Peter meet me in my office," Liam instructed.

There was a knock on the door. The reception nurse opened the door, poking her head inside the room. "Excuse me, Doctor, but you have a call on Line One."

Liam excused himself and crossed the room to the phone on the wall. "Doctor O'Dell," he answered.

"Hi, its me," a cheery voice on the other end replied.

"Oh, yes. Why, hello. Where are you?"

"This must be your professional side. You don't sound at all like the fabulous kisser I know." Silence. "I'm about an hour away. How's your day going?"

"I'll see you in a bit then. Are my directions all right?"

"They're fine. I'm actually making great time."

"Good. All right then. Call me if you have any problems." Liam hung up with out saying goodbye.

Josephine heard the line go dead and shook her head, as she closed the flap of her cell phone and placed it on the seat beside her. Liam's reaction to her call left her feeling embarrassed. She had obviously bothered him at an inappropriate time.

She started the car engine and drove out of the gas station back onto the highway. Isn't that just like a man, she thought. He told me to call him from the road. Annoyed, she reached forward to turn on the radio. As she drove back on to the interstate and with her car windows rolled down and wind whipping through her hair, she thought about Liam and decided she liked him better when he wasn't playing doctor.

His directions eventually brought her through the village of Waterbridge. She drove by slowly, watching shoppers meander along the sidewalks. Most of them carried crisp shopping bags with bold logos from the stores they had patronized.

Josephine pulled her car into a parking lot in front of the deli just as her cell phone rang.

"Hello?"

"Are you there yet?" It was her sister, Alex, calling from Cape Cod.

"Almost. I've pulled over for a pit stop." She had reached backward to grab a shoulder bag from the seat and was making some quick cosmetic repairs in the rearview mirror.

"I was hoping you were there already. I'm dying to know what you think of the daughter."

"Don't remind me, I'm nervous enough! You should see this place:

everybody's dressed to the nines. I'm wondering if I've brought the right clothes. And knowing I'll be staying in his house for two days...you know how I hate sleeping in any bed other than my own. Plus I get up every night to go to the bathroom..."

"You're nervous, aren't you?" Alex asked, picking up the hint of hysteria in her sister's voice.

"No kidding! What if his kid hates me?" Josephine was yanking the comb through her tangled hair, and trying single-handedly to put a leather hair band in it.

"She isn't going to hate you; you're great with kids. Robby loves you!"

"He's my nephew and he's five. This kid is almost fifteen. I have no idea how to relate to a teenager. I can't even relate to myself!"

"You'll be fine."

"Okay, if you say so. Listen, I've got to go. I'll try to sneak in a call to you over the weekend, if I can. I promised to call Marsha, too. She'll be grilling me for the complete rundown."

"Probably," Alex said. "You'll owe her that much for giving you the weekend off."

"Give my love to the guys, will you?"

"I will. Love you."

"Love you more," Josephine replied and disconnected the call.

Three miles outside the village she came to the last of the landmarks on Liam's directions before spotting *Quail Hollow Road.* As she drove slowly down the dirt road, she became aware of the serenity of her surroundings. As if they were forming a chapel, huge maple trees lined both sides of the road. Like fingers intertwining, their branches joined in the middle, creating a shaded cathedral effect as far down as the eye could see.

It was a mile's drive before Josephine saw the residences. Each one was built on several acres, with pine forests as backdrops. Some of the houses had brick or stone facings, multi-peaked roofs, and double or triple chimneys. All of them had magnificent windows which, when lit from inside, became beaconed paths of golden light which boldly shone across manicured lawns.

She came to a stone driveway with a white post at its entrance that had a lighted hanging sign which read *County Glen*.

The crunching of stone under the wheels sounded exceptionally loud in the silence of the evening as Josephine's car made its way down the winding driveway where an occasional ground lamp lit the path. At this early evening hour, the lights illuminated the dogwoods and wild shrubberies growing densely along both sides of the driveway.

Three turns and the driveway opened wide to expose the house: a two-story colonial, built of dark red brick, with a tall white circular porch supported by two pillars. Above it was a walk-out veranda accessible through double doors which Josephine guessed opened from the master bedroom. To the right was a three-car garage with what looked like an apartment above it. Later she would learn this was for the groundskeeper and his wife.

Liam came out the front door as Josephine was getting out of her car. He came to her quickly, enveloping her in a welcoming embrace. Removing her travel cases from the trunk, he took her hand and led her toward the house, apologizing for his brisk phone manner earlier that afternoon and inquiring after her drive.

They were crossing the front lawn when Josephine's eyes were drawn upward. There, silhouetted against the light of a bedroom window, stood a girl looking down. Assuming it was Meeghan, Josephine raised her free hand to wave, but the girl had disappeared.

Unease gave way to awe once Liam had led her inside the house. They stood in the large foyer with its high ceilings, circular staircase and antique brass chandelier while he gave a man's quick version of the outlay.

On the first floor was the formal living room and great room, with a two-way fireplace shared between them. On the same floor were also a dining room, kitchen, guest bath, and the library. Upstairs were four bedrooms, two of which had their own bathrooms, and two which shared an adjoining one.

He stepped aside, allowing Josephine to climb the white-spindled staircase with its mahogany hand rail. At the top was a wide landing.

She could see into both guest bedrooms, each softly lit and inviting. Liam offered either, and Josephine chose the blue room with its floral wallpaper and ornate double bed made of oak. It was an antique from the early nineteen hundreds and the focal point of the room. Its fluffy ice blue bedding and soft pillows called to her after the long drive.

Open windows, with delicate white lace curtains that shivered slightly in the evening breeze, beckoned her to look out the window to a swimming pool below, surrounded by a wrought iron gate, with a small cabana off to one side and a patio garden—all illuminated with ground lighting. Among the colorful wildflowers closing for the night were several stone sculptures barely seen among the sleepy blossoms.

"I love this room and its view," she breathed.

"I'm glad, but I think you should know it isn't as comfortable as mine," Liam hinted.

"No doubt."

"I'd show you Meeghan's room, but she is probably getting ready for dinner. Mrs. McGlynn baked a ham for tonight. I hope you're hungry."

"I am."

"Good. I love a girl with an appetite. I'll leave you to settle in then while I check on the other woman in my life. She has a tendency to drag her feet and is seldom ready on time."

"She's a woman," Josephine stated, shrugging her shoulders. "I brought her a present. I hope she will like it."

"It was kind of you to think of her. Settle in, and I will see you downstairs in a few minutes."

Alone, Josephine smiled to herself. Something warm and comfortable began flooding her senses. It was a feeling akin to being part of a family.

Meanwhile, down the hall behind her own bedroom door, a teenager was feeling quite differently. Hers was acute apprehension, brought on by the thought of meeting the first woman her father had ever invited into their home for a weekend.

ଓଃ

"Josephine Mitchell, meet Mary McGlynn, our housekeeper and my salvation. Without her my daughter and I would surely starve to death."

"How do you do," Josephine greeted the stout older woman standing in the dining room.

Mrs. McGlynn welcomed Josephine in her hearty Irish brogue, offering to help should she need anything during her stay. She then began a processional back and forth through the swinging door, transporting covered dishes one at a time from the kitchen to the dining table.

The tantalizing aromas reminded Josephine she hadn't eaten since breakfast. Liam was asking her something she didn't quite catch. "I'm sorry. What did you say?"

"I asked if you would like wine with your dinner."

"Please. A glass of wine would be perfect."

"Red, or white?"

"White, please." She held out her glass to be filled just as Meeghan entered the room.

"Sorry I'm late." A chunky girl of fourteen made a quick apology.

"Here she is!" Liam announced proudly. "Josephine, this is my daughter, Meeghan."

"Hello. I'm Josephine," she said, extending her hand in greeting. "You may call me Josie, if you like."

"Hello. I'm Meeghan, but everyone calls me Meggie."

"Then Meggie it will be," Josephine agreed, pleased to finally meet the child she had, until now, only imagined.

Meeghan's chin-length brown hair was held back with a navy blue headband which did nothing to flatter her round face. She was still dressed in her school uniform: a pleated plaid skirt which was snug on her, Josephine thought, and a navy sweater vest with a white blouse under it. She wore white knee socks, which seemed to strangle her hefty legs, and polished leather tie-up shoes.

When Meeghan had quietly taken her seat at the table, Mrs. McGlynn, like a mother hen, began portioning out the child's meal. She buttered her roll and placed another slice of ham and an extra serving of potatoes on top of what she had already put on her plate.

"That's enough, Mary, thank you. We can help ourselves," Liam said, dismissing her. "It all looks delicious."

"Aye, Doctor. I'll just go and ready the dessert then." Behind Liam's back, the cook gave Meeghan a wink and disappeared behind the swinging door.

"So, Meggie," Josephine began, "I've been looking forward to meeting you. I see you attend private school. Which one is it?"

"Saint Mary's."

"Do you like it? What grade are you in?"

"Ninth. I like it well enough."

Liam could tell he would have to help the conversational ball to roll. He said, "Meeghan's on the honor roll. She's an excellent student, aren't you, sweetheart?"

Meeghan, who had just buttered a roll and bitten into it, rolled her eyes. "Dad—"

"Don't talk with your mouth full," Liam corrected, "and eat your ham, please. It's better for you than the bread."

"I attended parochial school through eighth grade," Josephine said, spearing a forkful of fresh salad. "But then I switched to a public high school. I wasn't an honor roll student, but I seemed to excel in the arts. Which subject is it that you like best?"

"I like dance of any kind, but especially Celtic. I wanted to take lessons, but Dad won't let me."

Liam's brow was furrowed. "Let's not start this again."

"Well, it's true; you won't let me."

"You're right, I won't. Now finish your supper, please."

"I just remembered I brought gifts!" Josephine said gaily. "I believe Mrs. McGlynn put them on the sideboard."

Meeghan rose from her seat and walked over to fetch the presents, ceremoniously carrying them back to the table. She waited while Mrs. McGlynn served rice pudding with fresh whipped cream and topped with a ripe strawberry.

"My waistline could never survive in this household," Josephine remarked, dipping her spoon into the delectable dessert. "Everything is so delicious!" The cook seemed to visibly swell with pride, as her cheeks colored and she clucked her thanks.

Meeghan placed her father's package beside him. "Open yours first, Dad."

Liam look flustered. It was obvious by his expression he was not often the recipient of a gift. Removing the ribbon and wrapping, he opened a hardcover book of the paintings by Charles Wysocki. Inside was an inscription which read: *To Liam, with whom I share friends, food and flags. Thank you for an enjoyable weekend. Affectionately, Josephine.* He ran a hand over the book's smooth cover. "Thank you, Josie. It's a very thoughtful gift," he said. Reaching over the table, he nonchalantly placed his hand over hers and left it there.

Meeghan quickly finished her rice pudding and looked at her father questioningly.

"Yes," Liam said, "now you may open yours."

Moving the dish to one side, Meeghan placed her present before her. She began to unwrap it neatly, just as Mrs. McGlynn had taught her from early childhood. Inside the box was a black velvet bag tied at one end with a bow of gold silk cording. She untied the cord and the sack fell away to reveal a beautiful handcrafted hourglass.

"Oh, wow, this is so cool!"

"Turn it over," Josephine invited.

Meeghan turned it and sat mesmerized as she watched the soft sand began to thread its way from the top glass globe into the bottom one.

"It's a special hourglass, filled with the sands of time. It's supposed to be a reminder to the person who possesses it to fulfill their life's dream before time runs out."

"What do you say, Meeghan?" Liam reminded.

His daughter watched the sifting sand with rapt attention. To see her so enthralled was all the appreciation Josephine needed.

"Thank you, Josie. It's beautiful."

"I'm glad you like it."

"I do. I love it!"

Liam's gaze rested on his daughter for a moment. Then he said, "Okay, what do you say you bring these dishes in to the kitchen for Mrs. McGlynn?"

"I'm watching the sand," Meeghan answered.

"The sand will be running for an hour. It will take you exactly one minute to do as I asked. I'd like to visit alone with Josephine for a while."

"Can I use the computer when I'm done?"

"Yes, you may."

When Meeghan had cleared the table, she picked up the hourglass and came to stand between her father and their guest.

"Thank you again, Josie. This is really a neat gift."

"You're welcome I'm glad you like it."

Meeghan turned to her father and kissed him sweetly. "Night, Dad. Love you."

"I love you, too. Don't stay up too late, all right? I'm taking Josie for a walk down the road in the morning. If you want to join us, you'll have to get out of bed before noon."

"Not me!" Meeghan replied. She turned to Josephine and extending her hand. "Good night. It was very nice to meet you."

When they were alone, Josephine said to Liam, "She's sweet, and she has lovely manners, too!"

"Not bad for a teenager, I suppose."

"I think you've done a wonderful job of raising her, considering she has had no mother." She saw his face cloud over. "Forgive me. That was a bad choice of wording."

"It's all right. I understand what you were trying to say." Liam stood up from his chair and walked to the sideboard. "Can I interest you in a nightcap? I thought we'd sit a while in the family room."

"Sure."

Mary entered the dining room looking red-faced and overheated. She had finished the dishes and was untying her apron. "I'll be going now, Doctor, if there's no more you'll be wanting."

"No, Mary, thank you. Dinner was delicious, as always."

"Oh, yes, Mrs. McGlynn," Josephine joined in. "I can't remember when I have eaten such succulent ham. Perhaps some time you will teach me how to make a proper glaze?"

"There's nothing to it except for my secret ingredient. I add a touch of whiskey to the brown sugar."

Liam and Josephine retired to the family room where he closed the French doors behind them. After pouring brandy into two small crystal snifters, he invited Josephine to sit on the couch.

He placed his new book on the large coffee table in front of them.

"This will be nice to have here. Thank you again," he said. He leaned over and softly kissed her lips.

"You're welcome." Josephine leaned back against the soft cushions and slipped her feet out of their shoes. She waited, but nothing was said. "Is there something you would like to say to me?"

Liam had been staring into his tumbler, pondering his past and wondering how to broach the subject. He had never before shared the entire story with anyone, but found himself wanting to now. Josephine might never want to see him again after hearing it, but that was a chance he'd have to take. If they were to have a future together, it had to be based on truth and honesty.

He took a swallow of brandy, placed his glass on the table, and held his head in his hands. When he looked up he said, "I want to tell you about Meeghan's mother. Her name was Shannon. She worked part time in the library near the Rotunda Hospital, in Dublin, where I was completing my residency..."

CR

# CHAPTER *Four*

*Shannon was a college student majoring in Irish Folklore. She was a pretty girl of nineteen, tall and slender, with a fresh complexion, dark brown hair, and hazel eyes.*

*Her family lived in Kildare, and she was one of five children. When she left for college in Dublin, her parents permitted her to live with her Aunt Brigid, in her aunt's flat over the grocery store. Her aunt was an accomplished seamstress who kept long hours.*

*Shannon was shy and turned down most invitations from the Irish boys who tried to date her. Then one day she met Liam in the library, and their chance meeting changed her life completely.*

*Liam was older than Shannon by seven years. The fact that he was young, good-looking and American was enough for her to be attracted to him. But when she found out he was also a doctor, her crush on him turned to infatuation. Shannon went out of her way to be where Liam was. She looked for him at the library and sought him out at the local pubs when he was with his friends. Her innocence and willing spirit enticed him until eventually he stopped seeing other girls and began to date only her.*

*On a crisp Saturday afternoon in November, after spending a day together hiking in the countryside, Liam was bringing Shannon back home. Their ears, cheeks and hands were red with cold as they ran the last few blocks to her aunt's heated flat, where Shannon had promised him warm scones and hot tea. Once upstairs they threw off their coats, laughing and touching each other's warm necks with icy fingers. Shannon filled the teapot at the sink and carried it to the stove, igniting the burner with a match. While they waited for the water to boil, she and Liam began to kiss. At first their kisses were innocent and affectionate, gentle pecks and lingering nibbles. But then like a flame to dry leaves, their passion caught fire, carrying them away to a place they both longed to be.*

*Later neither of them would remember just how it was that they ended up naked on the futon. But afterwards the impact of what they had done, as well as the risk they had taken, occurred to them both and weighed heavily upon their consciences. Neither of them spoke about the possibility of pregnancy nor its outcome. They thought that perhaps if they didn't talk about it, it would not be so.*

*With eyes downcast, Liam and Shannon stood up and put their clothes back on in silence. They were unaware that, only moments before, they had created a daughter who was already beginning her journey toward life. Their own future together was about to evaporate as rapidly as the scalding steam escaping from the teapot on the stove.*

The clock on the mantel struck eleven. Josephine longed for bed, but her mind was alert. She managed to suppress an urge to yawn.

Liam was wide awake. "After we made love," he continued, "both of us realized the implication of not having used any birth control."

"Or self-control."

"You're right," he admitted sheepishly. "But it wasn't as though I wasn't going to stand by her. I told Shannon I was more than willing to marry her."

"If you made it sound as though it was your civic duty, no wonder she turned you down.

"Please, I know it's late and you're probably exhausted. But I want to finish telling you what happened. This is important to me." His forlorn expression brought out the boy in his handsome features.

"I'm sure it is; I'm sorry. Please go on."

"When Shannon found out she was pregnant, we were beside ourselves. Both of us knew full well our futures would be altered forever..."

*An enormous evergreen in the courtyard of The Rotunda Hospital in Dublin had been decorated with hundreds of brightly-colored lights, a festive contrast to the dreary December day.*

*Near the Christmas tree, on a cement bench outside the hospital's entrance, a young couple sat staring straight ahead.*

*Shannon had just confirmed their worst fear: she was pregnant. A gamut of emotions ran through them as they sat in silence wondering what to do. Their religious beliefs would never allow abortion, but the thought of going home to her family in this condition was more than terrifying to her.*

*Liam's reaction to the pregnancy was on a far more lucid level. He had already planned to ask Shannon to be his wife once he finished his residency. They could be married in Ireland, and then they would move back to America, where a promising position was already waiting for him. Now that they were expecting a child, it was simply a matter of pushing up the wedding date.*

*Liam held Shannon's hand and proposed to her, watching her face with eager anticipation. When he saw her worrisome expression somewhat soften, he assumed she would accept. But suddenly her eyes filled with tears.*

*Shannon poured out her heart to Liam. She professed her love and told him that although the thought of giving birth was frightening to her, she was sure she loved the baby growing inside her. But the mere thought of leaving Ireland and her family was a paralyzing one for her. And so, Shannon refused to marry Liam because she was sure that in her heart, she could never leave her homeland.*

*Emotionally exhausted, the couple pulled their hands apart, wondering what to do and where to go. In the twilight of the evening, with the Christmas lights casting a color wheel across their stilled forms, they sat: father, mother-to-be, and unborn child. At this most holy time of year Shannon and Liam were reminded of a time, centuries before them, when another couple had wandered into Bethlehem in search of a safe place for themselves and their baby who would soon be born.*

Liam now had Josephine's full attention. She was eager to know how it was that Liam ended up bringing Meeghan home with him.

"As soon as the holidays were over," Liam told her, "Shannon and I asked the parish priest to come to her Aunt's place one evening..."

*Father Joseph Ryan heard the confessions of a young couple ridden with guilt and conviction. It did not help the situation to see Shannon's Aunt Brigid, a normally jubilant woman, crying uncontrollably. Father Ryan was not only a religious man, but an understanding one, as well. He told them that while they needed to acknowledge the sin they had committed, it was also important they credit themselves with the responsible and Christian decision to give their child a life it deserved.*

*He reminded them of the absolution granted them during confession and, more importantly, of God's forgiveness.*

*In the end it was decided that Shannon would stay with her aunt until the baby was born. Her family would be told that she had been invited to take part in an internship which required her to remain in Dublin for an indefinite amount of time. Liam would be responsible for Shannon's prenatal care and for the delivery of their child.*

*The priest blessed them and then took his leave. Shannon and Liam sat down on the futon where it had all begun. They held on to each other and cried.*

*In August, when the time came, Liam coached Shannon through her labor, safely delivering their daughter into the world. Father Ryan baptized the child Meeghan Kathleen.*

*As soon as his residency ended, Liam flew home to America to begin his new job while obtaining a falsified birth certificate to take back to Ireland.*

*Three months later he was once again in Ireland. But when he flew back to New York, this time he carried in his arms a new citizen of the United States.*

Later, Josephine lay awake with her eyes open. The sleigh bed with its feather mattress and abundance of cloud-like bedding enveloped her in luxury, and her body cried out for rest, yet her mind would not stop spinning.

The ground lights from the gardens below cast a soft creamy glow in the room, creating shadowed shapes of the furniture, which loomed over her like bodyguards.

She lay on her side, watching the lace curtains perform a hypnotic dance as the evening air moved through them on its way to whisper across her skin. It gently caressed her face, wooing her to close her eyes.

Finally, she felt her body let go, sinking into a slumbering abyss, where her fitful dreams carried her at lightning speed to the green hills of Ireland.

CR

# CHAPTER *Five*

Beneath the drawn shade, the slot of open window permitted a strip of early morning sunlight to stretch across the room like a laser beam. It cast its golden warmth in ribbons across the bed where Josephine lay and inched its way toward her face as the hour advanced. Robins and sparrows chirped noisily outside, and in the distance someone was mowing a lawn, jarring the neighborhood to consciousness.

Only half awake, Josephine reached out from under the warm covers to feel for the wrist watch she had left on the table beside the bed. She opened one sleepy eye, grabbed the watch, and saw it was after eight o'clock. Thinking she might be holding up breakfast, she kicked back the covers and forced herself out of bed.

Before long she was downstairs, dressed in a pair of khaki Capri pants and a navy blue T-shirt. Across her shoulders she had tied a white cotton sweater to match the new sneakers she had brought especially for the weekend.

She opened the pair of dark sunglasses and placed them on top of her head as she followed the sound of the television coming from the family room, where she and Liam had talked until after midnight.

Mrs. McGlynn had cleared away the empty cordial glasses and fluffed the couch cushions. Meeghan, who was sprawled out on the couch in a pair of red cotton pajamas patterned with black Scotties, barely turned from the show she was watching when Josephine entered the room. Her hair was disheveled and her eyes held telltale signs of having just risen from bed.

"Good morning," Josephine greeted.

Meeghan did not look up. "Morning," she mumbled, taking a spoonful of cold cereal from the bowl on her lap.

"Your guest bed was so comfortable; I slept like a princess in a fairy tale!"

"Mrs. McGlynn said to tell you she has breakfast set in the dining room."

"Thanks. Where's your dad?"

"He got called in," Meeghan told her, taking a bite from a glazed doughnut. "He's delivering twins." She picked up the remote and began flipping through the channels, no longer interested in the movie. "Usually I'm in bed till noon on a Saturday, but Dad said I have to entertain you till he gets back."

"I see." Josephine was unsure of what to do with a teenager and an indefinite amount of time. "Well, let me get some coffee and think on this a minute." She came back with a small dish of fresh fruit, half a bagel with cream cheese and a steaming mug of coffee. Meeghan had finished the last of the doughnut and was licking her fingers.

"What would you say to showing me around?" Josephine asked, sipping her coffee. "I saw some interesting houses as I was driving up the road yesterday. I'd enjoy seeing them in the daylight."

"We could take the bikes," Meeghan said, "that is if you can ride a boy's bike."

"Sure, why not?"

"Good. You can use Dad's. I have to shower first and make my bed." She stood up and stretched. Josephine noticed she had painted her toenails bright pink.

"I like your toes," she commented. "What color is that?"

"It's called *Flirt*." Meeghan wiggled her toes. "I wanted to paint my fingernails, too, but they're in pretty bad shape." She looked admiringly at Josephine's neat, rounded fingernails with their French manicure. "I like your French."

"If you want, I can paint yours for you when we get back from our ride."

"That's okay. I'd rather go swimming."

"Isn't it a little early in the season?"

"We have a heated pool."

"But I didn't bring a suit."

"No problem. We can go downtown. You can buy one there."

Josephine sighed and took a gulp of coffee. Instinct told her this was going to be a very long day.

An occasional stone shot out from under the tires of their bicycles as the two bikers pedaled their way along the unpaved length of Quail Hollow Road. Like a gossip columnist, Meeghan described each family to Josephine, as well as the goings on in their households. Their ride was long and languid except when the road inclined. Then they were forced to dismount and walk the bikes uphill.

As they approached the steepest climb in the road, Josephine called a challenge to see which one of them could pedal uphill longer without getting off the bike. They stood up and pumped with all their strength, pulling their weight against the support of the handlebars, until they could stand the strain no longer.

Josephine was the first to surrender. She jumped off her bike and stood panting, her chest heaving with exertion as she shouted ahead, "Go, Meggie, go!"

Meeghan put all her strength into the climb, standing up to pedal until the muscles in her legs ached and her lungs burned, refusing to dismount until she had made it to the top of the hill. Only then did she jump off the bike, gulping for air while waving one hand above her head. "I did it!" she shouted.

Josephine gave a congratulatory *thumb's up* sign as she joined Meeghan at the top of the hill. They stood together with heaving chests.

"I've never, ever been able to do that!" Meeghan gasped.

"Invigorating," Josephine muttered, wiping the perspiration from her forehead.

They walked their bikes side by side, their heart rates returning to normal as they headed back home.

The house next door to *County Glen* was a rambling two-story dwelling with stone facing and an attached greenhouse. This was the home of David and Laura Barnard and their three children. David owned one of the top construction companies in the area, and his crews had developed Quail Hollow Road. Scott and Jeremy Barnard were nine-year old twins, and their sister, Amelia, was Meeghan's best friend.

Laura Barnard was outside with the twins playing softball on the front lawn. Their beagle, Huckleberry, repeatedly ran under foot, barking his way around the bases as he tripped the boys and playfully nipped at Laura's ankles.

Scott batted the ball in the direction of the two riders coming up the road. Laura spotted them and flagged Meeghan down with a wave. She knew that Liam was expecting a lady friend for the weekend, and Laura was anxious to get a good look at the woman who had finally managed to turn his head.

Josephine and Meeghan stood waiting, holding their bikes at their sides, while Laura made her way across the expanse of manicured lawn. She was an effervescent woman—short and petite, with a pixie haircut. She wore denim shorts and a baseball jersey, and Josephine thought she looked more like a babysitter than the children's mother.

"Hi, Meggie, you're up early!" Laura waited for Meeghan to make introductions; and when she didn't, she extended her hand. "How do you do; I'm Laura Barnard."

"Josephine Mitchell; pleased to meet you."

"I had heard that you were coming this weekend. How are you enjoying your stay so far?"

"Very much, thanks to Meggie. She's taking good care of me."

"And I see Liam got out of exercising, or is he at the hospital this morning?"

"He's delivering twins," Meeghan said. "Where's Amelia?"

"She's still sleeping." Laura turned back to Josephine. "Twins, eh? It sounds as though you might be on your own for a while. If you need anything while Liam's gone, feel free to call."

Josephine took an immediate liking to Laura. She felt that given the chance, the two of them could easily become friends.

"You'll enjoy being with this one," Laura said, cupping her hand under Meeghan's rounded chin. "She's an intricate part of our family. My husband thinks we should adopt her."

The twins, who until now had been playing amicably together, broke into a squabble. Scott shoved his brother, and the two dropped to the ground and began rough-housing and arguing. Huckleberry tried his best to get in the thick of it, barking and jumping on the backs of the brothers as they tumbled and twisted like laundry in a dryer. Laura was about to excuse herself and intervene, when the door to the greenhouse opened and her husband stepped outside.

David Barnard resembled a linebacker. In a rumbling undertone he spoke to his sons. Immediately the boys got up from the ground and brushed themselves off. Their father rumbled once more, and the boys scrambled to retrieve the bat, ball and gloves from the lawn. They then shuffled off towards the garage with Huckleberry in tow, his long tail wagging like a metronome.

"Sweetheart," Laura called out. "Can you come here? There's someone I want you to meet."

David nodded but remained where he was until he was sure the boys had followed through on his orders. Then he lumbered over, removing his work gloves as he walked.

"Honey," Laura said, "this is Josephine Mitchell. Do you remember Amelia told us she was coming?"

"Yes, of course. Hello there," David said, pumping Josephine's hand in greeting. He turned to Meeghan. "And how's our girl today? Are you behaving?"

"Naturally," Meeghan quipped. "Guess what I just did?"

"I give up. What did you do?"

"I rode all the way up that steep hill—the one before the Remingtons' house—without getting off my bike!"

"You don't say." David appeared impressed. "Too bad Amelia is being such a slouch this morning. If she had gotten out of bed, she could have gone with you."

"Can I get you something cold to drink?" Laura offered. "Iced tea, soda, water?" It was nearing noon, and the day was unusually warm for the time of year.

"Thank you," Josephine said, "but we need to go into town so I can buy a bathing suit. I didn't think to bring one with me."

"I have several. You're welcome to borrow one, if you like. I'm sure any of them would fit you."

"Thanks so much; it's kind of you to offer. But I need to get a new one anyway. I don't own a suit I dare to be seen in."

Laura laughed. "Does any woman, other than a runway model, ever like the way she looks in a bathing suit?"

"If you ladies will excuse me," David said, "that's my cue. I learned long ago never to hang around when a woman's conversation turns to body shapes or weight."

"We need to get going, too," Josephine said. "It was nice meeting you both."

"And you, Josephine." Laura said.

"Please, call me Josie."

"I hope we'll see you again, Josie." Laura turned and gave Meeghan a hearty hug. "Goodbye, Sweetie. Amelia is going to be sorry she missed you."

"I'll see her later, remember? Dad said she could sleep over tonight. He's taking Josie out to dinner to that new Italian restaurant."

"You mean Modena's?" Laura asked. "Oh, Josie, you're going to love it. David and I went there two weeks ago. It was delicious! Have a great time. After delivering twins, Liam is going to need to unwind tonight!"

When they were back on their bikes, Meeghan spoke of her best friend's talent as an equestrian and of the many competitions she had won. Amelia's bedroom had nearly a hundred ribbons hanging on the wall, and Meeghan recited all four colors and which placing they represented. Then she told Josephine of Amelia's accident when she was ten years old: how she had fallen from her horse and hit her head. The impact had severed the optic nerve so that Amelia had permanently lost the vision in her left eye.

Meeghan repeated the incident to Josephine, describing Amelia's accident with its resulting handicap as if it was no more than a scratch on her best friend's knee.

# CHAPTER *Six*

There was a clothing shop in town running a two-for-one sale. Josephine came out of the dressing room modeling what seemed to Meeghan to be a hundred different styles before settling on both a white halter top one-piece suit and a black strapless one.

The saleslady suggested a pair of expensive Italian leather sandals, but Josephine was feeling just lighthearted and carefree enough to choose ridiculous-looking rubber flip-flops with silk daisies on top.

Back at the house, she checked her cell phone for any missed messages and noticed her sister had called. She pressed the numbers on the key pad and waited for an answer while she began undressing.

"There you are," Alex answered, expecting the call.

"Hi. This is the first chance I've had to call you. We were out shopping. How are you?" Josephine huffed, as she struggled out of her clothing with her one free hand.

"I'm fine, but you sound winded. What's up?"

"I'm trying to change into a bathing suit. We're about to go swimming."

"It must be warm there. Are you having a good time? How's Liam?"

"I couldn't tell you. He has been at the hospital all morning delivering twins."

"Ah, such is the life of a doctor," Alex mused. "Keep it in mind. They're never home, you know."

"So I'm told. It's all right, though, Meggie's here to keep me company. We've had quite the time so far."

"Is she okay? Does she seem to like you? How's the house?"

"Yes. I think so. And gorgeous!" Josephine fired off the three answers. "It's enormous, and I'm staying in the most beautiful guest room you'd ever want to see."

"Guest room? I thought you'd be..."

"Not yet," Josephine cut in.

"What are you waiting for?"

"I'm waiting for it to be the right time. Besides, there's Meggie to consider."

"You're right. I forgot she's too old to pull the wool over her eyes."

"How are the guys?"

"They're fine. Rob took Robby to soccer practice."

"Good. That means you've got a short reprieve. Enjoy it. Listen, let me go," Josephine urged. "I've got to get down to the pool; Meggie's waiting for me."

"Will you listen to yourself? You sound like a mother."

"She's a good kid. I like her."

"That's good, especially if you and Liam end up together."

"I can't think that far ahead. At this moment I'm not thinking past the sunshine outside. I'm being taken to dinner tonight; I want a little color."

"Nice. Have a good time. I'll talk to you when you get back home. Be careful and drive safely tomorrow, you hear?"

"I will. Kiss your guys for me!"

Josephine put the phone back on the dresser. She put away her clothes and quickly donned the black strapless suit, covering herself with a short cotton robe. Slipping into the silly-looking rubber flip-flops with the big daisies, she pulled her hair into a makeshift ponytail and headed down the stairs.

On the way past the dining room she entered it in hopes of finding something to eat. Mrs. McGlynn had placed a plate of finger sandwiches along with a brightly-colored bowl of fruit on the sideboard. Josephine reached for a shiny green apple off the top, taking a clean bite of it as she made her way into the kitchen. There she took two bottled waters from the refrigerator before heading out into the afternoon sunshine.

Meeghan was sitting upright in a lounge chair, eating potato chips from an open bag on her lap. Josephine handed her a cold bottle of water. Meeghan shaded her eyes with one hand and reached up to take it from her. She noticed the apple. "You eat very healthy, don't you?"

"I try to."

Suddenly Meeghan wasn't hungry anymore. She rolled the chip bag closed and put it on the snack table beside her. When she stood up, the purple two piece bathing suit she wore showed signs of straining around her hips and across her back. Although her legs were long, her full thighs touched in the middle.

She walked to the edge of the pool and hesitated only a minute before taking a perfect dive. She surfaced and began swimming laps. Once she reached the far end of the pool, she held on and waited to catch her breath before making her way back again. She kept her strokes even, driven by her envy of Josephine and her father's attraction to her. She forced herself to complete five laps before climbing out of the pool, breathless. Wrapping a large terrycloth towel around herself, Meeghan again headed for the lounge chairs where Josephine was already stretched out, sunning.

She removed her towel and spread it over the chair before lying down on it. She purposely turned her back to Josephine, who lay with eyes closed behind a pair of dark sunglasses, unaware that the young girl had tears of frustration in her eyes.

Several minutes later, the wrought-iron gate behind them opened and a skinny girl with lanky blond hair walked through. "Hey," she called. "My mom told me you'd be at the pool. I heard I missed the marathon bike ride this morning!" She was speaking to Meeghan, but eyeing the woman lying in the chair beside her.

"Oh, yeah, it was a real Olympic performance," Meeghan moaned. "My dad had to go to the hospital early this morning and said I had to keep *her* company." She inclined her head in Josephine's direction, thinking she was dozing.

Josephine was, in fact, wide awake and had been watching the two girls from behind her dark glasses. She recognized Amelia by her one expressionless eye that almost seemed dead-looking, like a shark's eye. It was an unfortunate mar in the girl's otherwise flawless beauty.

"You don't have to stay, you know." The sound of Josephine's voice startled the two teens. "I'm perfectly capable of being here alone if you'd like to go do something else." She raised her dark glasses, pushing them up on to her head. "Hi, there, I'm Josie."

"Sorry." Meeghan apologized. "This is Amelia."

"Hello," Amelia mumbled.

"Want to go swimming?" Meeghan invited.

"No thanks." Amelia appeared paralyzed. "Let's go up to your room."

"Okay." Meeghan rose and took her towel from the chair and grabbed the unfinished bag of potato chips to take with them.

"Have a good time," Josephine called out. "It was nice to meet you, Amelia."

Once behind the bedroom door, Amelia squealed, "Oh, Meggie! What if your dad actually marries her?"

"I don't know...she doesn't seem so bad."

"You'll have a *stepmother*, hello?" Amelia sat on the rug and leaned against Meeghan's bed. "She'll start telling you what to do and stuff. And when you ask your father for something that she doesn't think you should have, she'll make him agree with her!"

Meeghan had gone into the bathroom to change. Amelia continued to talk on the other side of the door. "And the very worst thing is that she will act like she's your real mother!"

Meeghan came out of the bathroom dressed in jeans that were too tight for her and an oversized shirt. Her towel and bathing suit lay in a damp rumpled ball on the bathroom floor, despite Mrs. McGlynn's constant harping on tidiness.

"So, what's wrong with that? It's not like I have a mother who cares about me." She sat down beside her friend and lowered her head. Her brown hair covered enough of her face that Amelia could not tell how much the remark had hurt.

"Yes, but you *do* have one, she just happens to live in Ireland," Amelia insisted. "And maybe one day your dad will agree to take you there to meet her, but your stepmother won't think that's a good idea. Maybe she'll be jealous and won't let you go."

"I don't know...Josie doesn't seem so bad, and my mother hasn't exactly made a point of getting to know me. Believe me, I'll watch out for myself and my dad. No woman's going to come between us." She moved close to her friend and took hold of her hand. "But I must admit that the idea of having a woman here to talk to about certain things. You know, like girl things. Sometimes I think I'd like that."

"What about Mrs. McGlynn?"

"She's too old!"

"Okay, but don't say I didn't warn you." Amelia noticed the hourglass on the dresser. "What's that?"

"Pick it up," Meeghan invited, baiting her.

Amelia reached up and brought the hourglass to the floor. She set it between them, turning it over and watching as the soft sand sifted through the glass orbs.

"It's beautiful! Where did you get it?"

"It was a gift."

"Wow! This is so cool! Who's it from?"

"Josie."

Amelia's mouth hung open, as the sand continued to pass the time.

ᏋᏒ

# CHAPTER *Seven*

Modena's had become *the* place to dine. Its reputation was widespread as a classy, affordable bistro, offering a menu of authentic recipes from various regions of Italy.

Seated at an intimate corner table for two, Josephine could feel Liam's admiring glances bringing the familiar blush from her cheeks down to her chest. She sipped from a glass of chilled Pinot Grigio while fidgeting slightly under his intense scrutiny.

"Chanel Number Five?" he asked, sniffing the air. Josephine nodded, pleased that he could identify her favorite scent.

"You look fantastic!" He leaned over to kiss the curve of her neck. As his lips touched her bare skin, he inhaled her perfume. Its headiness made him wish they could skip dinner so he could take her home to his bed.

Josephine did indeed look attractive in a pair of wide-legged black crepe pants with a matching box jacket cropped to the waist. She left the jacket unbuttoned with a sleeveless white camisole underneath. She wore a choker of black pearls and earrings to match, perfect accessories to complement the healthy glow of her skin, which had been kissed by the sun earlier in the day.

The wine steward refilled their glasses and a waiter placed their entrees in front of them with dramatic flair. The chef had artistically arranged a rack of lamb with rosemary and port wine reduction for Liam and chicken Florentine for Josephine.

"I feel terrible about today," Liam apologized, as he cut into a tiny lamb chop which had been roasted to perfection. "Those twins weren't due for another two weeks. I had a list of things for us to do together."

"Not to worry; I was fine. Meeghan and I had a nice time together, truly. She's a great kid."

"She is that, but she can get me crazy, too."

"Can't all children?"

"Is it because she is a teenager," he querried, "or because she's a girl?"

"I'm curious: what is your objection to her taking dance lessons?" Josephine asked.

"I have no objection, but I also have no time to orchestrate an extra-curricular agenda for her. It's unfortunate Meggie misses out on some things because she has had no mother, but I'm doing the best I can." There was a hint of agitation in his voice.

Unwilling to chance ruining the evening, Josephine invited Liam to sample her entrée.

"Just a piece," he said, accepting her offering. "M-m-m, that's great." He wiped his mouth on a white linen napkin and moved his chair closer to hers. Together they sat leaning intimately toward one another, more hungry for conversation than for food, and both believing this weekend to be some sort of turning point in their whirlwind courtship.

Sometime later, their waiter presented the dessert choices, which Josephine declined. Liam ordered two cappuccinos and a dish of ginger gelato to share. When it was placed in front of them, they repeatedly dipped two silver spoons into the frozen cream, savoring the pleasure like teenagers at a soda shop. And so it was that they failed to notice the curvaceous thirty-year old brunette, who was turning heads as she passed by, until she approached their table and stood tall with one hand on a slender hip. When he saw who it was, Liam quietly put down his spoon.

"Well, well, the woman said with contempt. "If it isn't Doctor O'Dell. I wondered why I haven't heard from you. Now I can see why."

She wore a red spandex mini dress that flattered her long legs accentuated by a pair of black sling-back high heels. Her brown hair tumbled in dark thick curls to her shoulders, and her eyes were dark and brooding. Her fingernails were painted the same shade of red as her dress; touches of gold jewelry flashed from her wrist, throat and ear lobes. Josephine thought the woman was centerfold material.

Liam's expression became serious. "Josie, this is Michelle."

Josephine nodded politely, but her heart began to race. So this is *the nurse*. Josephine made an immediate comparison between herself and the woman in red and came away feeling at a disadvantage.

"What brings you here?" Liam asked, taking a sip of his coffee and trying to appear relaxed. He had always disliked confrontations; intuition warned him to brace himself.

"I'm here with the girls from third shift," Michelle said, her red lips set in a thin line.

Josephine started to get up. "If you both will excuse me..."

"You don't have to leave," Liam said, reaching for her hand. "I have nothing to say to Michelle that you can't hear."

"Well I have something to say to *you*, Liam." Michelle leaned forward to place her hands on the table. Her knuckles were white with tension and her face flushed with indignation.

"You used me, and you lied to me—telling me you needed to devote more time to your daughter!" Her lower lip began to tremble, and her expression changed from resentment to self-pity. "I believed you, even when the rumors about her went around the hospital." Michelle shot her chin towards Josephine.

"Michelle, this isn't the time...," Liam warned.

"And now here you are," she barreled on. "Is this what you call spending time with your *daughter*? I don't think so!" Her eyes swam with tears.

Josephine watched to see if the woman's makeup would smear, but it remained perfectly applied through the salty rivulets that fell unchecked.

Michelle looked at Josephine. "I know none of this is your fault, but I love this man."

"You're out of line, Michelle!" Liam snapped under his breath.

"What's wrong? You don't want your girlfriend here to know the truth?"

"No need to explain; I understand—" Josephine said, trying to ease the tension.

"No, you don't understand! You can't possibly understand! But then, why should you? This has nothing to do with you. This is between Liam and me."

Liam's eyes darkened. "There is nothing between you and me, and this has *everything* to do with Josephine." Michelle flinched as if she had been slapped, but Liam kept his tone. "You and I dated. We had what we had. We never spoke about commitment; there was no profession of love on my part. I'm sorry you're hurt—that was never my intention. But I resent your coming over here attempting to ruin our evening."

Michelle looked incredulous. "You're really amazing, Liam, do you know that?" She looked at Josephine. "I wish I could say it was nice meeting you." Then she turned and walked away, holding her head high with as much dignity as she could muster.

At first neither Liam nor Josephine spoke. Finally Liam opened his mouth to say something, but Josephine put up her hand. She had heard enough for one evening. His apologies could do nothing to make her feel better about meeting the woman he had been sleeping with; and at this moment, her only wish was that she was back in Clapton.

Liam paid the bill and the two of them left the restaurant. As they drove from the parking lot, they could see Michelle standing at the far end of the veranda, staring out into the darkness of the night.

The ride home was silent, both of them lost in their own thoughts. Liam parked his Mercedes in the garage and came around to open Josephine's door. She accepted his hand as she stepped out, but pushed him away when he tried to take her in his arms.

"Josie...," he groaned, but she put up her hand and gently shook her head.

"Liam, please, I'm really tired." She walked toward the house ahead of him.

They paused in the foyer, avoiding each other's eyes. Both of them realized that the weekend they had so looked forward to had fallen far short of their expectations.

"Thank you for dinner. The food was excellent," she said in a voice void of emotion.

Liam looked tired and worn. It had been a long day for him, and Michelle's scene at the restaurant had unsettled his nerves. Yet it was important to him that Josephine not be upset before going to bed.

"I don't suppose I could interest you in joining me for a midnight swim in the heated pool? It may help us both to relax."

"Thank you, no. Actually, I'm not feeling very well, and I should get some sleep. I've got a long drive tomorrow."

Liam reached out to hold her by the shoulders. Josephine could feel the soothing heat of his hands through the fabric of her jacket. He searched her eyes with his own and she was moved by the sincerity in his expression. The depth of his gaze seemed to penetrate her soul.

"This is not where I wanted to be when I told you this," he said, "but I care for you, Josephine. What I had with Michelle...,"

"Not tonight, Liam, please," she moaned. "I'm going to bed now." She kissed him lightly on the mouth and began mounting the stairs. "Goodnight."

For the second time in less than an hour, Liam O'Dell watched a woman turn her back on him and walk away. The first one had never mattered much to him. But it was different with the second one. The second one mattered a great deal.

The next morning, Josephine was out of bed early. She pulled aside the lace curtains and lifted the shade only to be greeted by an overcast sky. Perfect for driving, she thought. She was showered and dressed for church before Liam, or Meeghan, had wakened. Her bags had been packed and stood in readiness for the trip home.

She folded back the bedding, still warm and smelling faintly of her perfume and then placed her used bath towels in a folded stack on the bathroom counter. With a last look around the room she sighed and lifted her luggage to carry it down the stairs.

Mrs. McGlynn had just finished laying out an assortment of breakfast muffins and fruits when Josephine walked into the dining room.

"Good morning," Mary greeted, looking fresh and tidy in a gray skirt and white blouse with a starched white apron tied around her ample middle. "And why are you packed so early? Will you tell me that?"

"I'm going to need an early start for home."

"Won't you be going to church with the doctor then?" She eyed the younger woman warily, daring her to defy the Sabbath.

"Yes, of course I am. What time is mass?"

"That would be the nine o'clock. Patrick and I go on Saturdays," she added, making sure Josephine knew she and her husband had fulfilled their own spiritual obligations.

"I guess I have some time to kill," Josephine replied, looking at her watch.

"Will you have a cup of coffee while you wait?"

"Coffee would be lovely, thank you." She gratefully accepted a mug of the strong brew. "I'll wait in the garden until the others are ready."

Outside Josephine walked the perimeter of the garden, making a professional assessment of its horticultural layout as she sipped her coffee. Occasionally she stooped to smell a fragrant flower, or to fondle a fat tiny bud ready to burst into bloom. She headed for the lilac trees, the age of which explained their size. There she encountered Patrick McGlynn, on a stepladder, cutting boughs of the fragrant lavender blossoms. As he clipped the branches, they fell to the ground where he could gather them in an enormous wicker basket.

Patrick stopped what he was doing when he saw Josephine approaching. He had already seen his seventieth birthday, but he could still appreciate a beautiful woman when he saw one.

"Top 'o the morn'n to you, Mr. McGlynn!" Josephine called out.

"Well I might say, that 'tis a fine Irish greeting for one as old as me, miss," replied the gardener, smiling broadly. He was proud of having all of his original teeth, unlike his wife who had been wearing dentures for years. "You're up early then. Was my ladder making too much of a racket out here?"

"Not at all," she assured him. She liked this gentle man and his easy, friendly manner. "I have a long drive home this morning after we come back from church."

Patrick McGlynn smiled again, his weathered face breaking into many lines as he handed her a generous bunch of lilac blooms. Josephine buried her nose among the blossoms and inhaled deeply.

"Thank you, these are lovely!"

"Just have the missus wrap the stems good and tight, and they will stay fresh till you get home."

"I'll do that, thank you."

"If I don't see you before you leave today, miss, I'm wishing you a safe trip back and hoping we'll see you soon again."

"Thank you," she replied, embracing the fragrant bouquet and holding it close to her chest.

"Godspeed, miss." The old man returned to the pruning, sure that his wife was wondering what was taking him so long.

As she walked to the house, Josephine noticed Amelia walking across the lawn toward home, her overnight bag slung over her arm. This meant Liam and Meeghan would be downstairs shortly, and the three of them would be going to church together. She waved to Amelia, who ignored the greeting and kept on walking. Josephine's thoughts turned to the night before. She couldn't help but relive the scene between Liam and Michelle, its memory instantly causing her to feel sick inside. There was no way she could be persuaded to stay for breakfast after mass. She quickened her step and entered the house, anxious to have church over with so she could be on her way.

*I know none of this is your fault, but I love this man, too.* Michelle's face loomed large in her mind. She left her coffee mug in the kitchen sink, grateful that Mrs. McGlynn made no more conversation other than an offer to secure the lilacs in water for the long drive to Clapton.

In the foyer Josephine found Meeghan standing on the staircase, nervously nibbling a thumbnail and holding one hand across her stomach. "I've got a headache and really bad cramps," she said softly, gripping the banister dramatically. "Dad's going to think I'm lying to get out of going to church."

"I doubt that." Josephine guided her gently by the elbow, leading her up the stairs with an assurance she did not entirely feel. "Did you take anything for it?"

"Not yet."

They entered her bedroom where she helped Meeghan back to bed then went to the medicine cabinet and located the bottle of Ibuprofen. Shaking two from the bottle, she filled a glass with water from the tap. Seeing the girl lying in bed carried Josephine back in time to her own youth when her mother nursed whatever ailed her. Her eyes went soft with remembrance of years gone by. She heard Liam outside, honking the car horn, and visualized him looking at his watch. She hurried to the task. "Take these; they will make you feel better." She placed the pills in Meeghan's hand and handed her the water. Outside Liam tapped his car horn again.

"What are you going to tell Dad?"

"I'm going to tell him the truth. I'm sure he will believe you don't feel well." She raised the bedding and covered Meeghan's shoulders. "Rest and take it easy. I'll come to see you before I leave for home, okay?"

"When will you be coming back?" The look in her eyes said she hoped it would be soon.

As upset as she was with Liam, Josephine could not take her emotion out on his daughter. "As soon as I can," she answered. "I promise."

The car horn sounded a third time, this time with greater urgency. She hurried down the stairs and out the front door. Though they were going to be late for mass, Josephine was fairly sure that after the scene at the restaurant the night before, Liam wouldn't be in a position to complain about much.

"What is taking so long?" he asked when she got into the car. "Where's Meggie?"

"She won't be joining us; woman problems."

"Lately I've had a few of those, myself."

Josephine watched with boredom as the scenery sped by her window. Perhaps prayer will be a good thing right about now, she thought, resting her chin on the palm of her hand and feeling the constraints of a visit gone sour.

# CHAPTER *Eight*

At dinner that evening, Meeghan waited for her father's interrogation over missing mass, but Liam only asked how she was feeling.

"I'm better, thanks, but was Josie all right when she left today?"

"I think so. Why wouldn't she be?" Liam carved the small roast that had been set before him. He helped his daughter to a juicy slice before carving himself a generous slab.

"I don't know. She looked anxious to leave, like she couldn't wait to go."

"She had a long drive ahead of her and wanted to get back home before dark. Why?" he hedged. "Did she say anything to you?"

"No, but when I asked when I'd see her again, she said she wasn't sure." She corralled the buttered peas on her plate into a pile, then dragged her fork through the center, sending them scattering. Two rolled off her plate onto the white tablecloth. "It didn't sound like she wants to come back too soon."

Liam retrieved the peas and popped them in his mouth. "She'll be back."

"How can you be sure?"

"Because," he said, wearing a foolish grin, "we're like two peas in a pod!"

Earlier that day, Liam had tried calling Josephine's cell phone while she was on the road, but she wouldn't pick up. He waited to hear the beep. "Hi, it's me," he said, unsure of what message to leave. "Just making sure you're not lost out there somewhere. Call me, okay? I want to know you're all right and that you haven't taken any wrong turns. Okay. Bye."

After supper, he had tried her home phone. It rang four times before the recording clicked on. "Hi, it's me again. I'm figuring you should have gotten there by now. I'm hoping you went out for something to eat, but I'm starting to get worried. Please call and let me know that you got home safely. Okay, bye."

His third try was at nine o'clock that night. He heard three rings before Josephine picked up the receiver at her end.

"Hello?"

"It's me," Liam said, sounding annoyed. "Why didn't you call me?"

"I was busy unpacking and doing laundry, and I had a few calls to return when I got home."

"Yeah, well it would have been considerate if one of those calls had been to me!"

Silence.

"I've been worried. Meggie was, too."

"How is she?"

"Fine. She's fine. She wants to know when she's going to see you again. She felt you left here upset."

"That was pretty intuitive of her. What did you tell her?"

"I said you'd be coming back—that she would be seeing you again very soon."

"I'm not sure about that, Liam."

For several seconds, neither one spoke. The relationship was fragile, and the wrong words right now could send it shattering. Liam took a chance.

"Josie, please hear me out. I had such great expectations for this weekend, and maybe that was wrong of me, but I wanted it to be perfect for you, for *us*. Instead, it went all wrong with my getting called into delivery, and then Michelle showing up at the restaurant. When you left today, I felt as though the weekend had been a complete bust. But then I got to thinking, and I realized it was really good after all, the way it turned out."

"I don't understand. What was *good* about Michelle spoiling the one and only part of the weekend we had alone together?"

"It's good because now you don't have to wonder about her anymore. You heard it firsthand when I told her there was nothing between us."

As Josephine listened, her resolve began to crumble. Her intention was to keep a stiff upper lip, to give Liam the cool treatment at least for a few days. But he was saying what she wanted to hear. And what he was telling her now she had only heard him whisper in her dreams.

"Josie, I love you; you are perfect for me. And if you will give me another chance, I promise do everything within my power to make you happy. What do you say, can we try this again? Josie? Are you still there?"

She never heard the question, for she was holding the phone away from her ear, shaking her head in euphoric disbelief.

☙

Their summer was eventful, with weather that ran hot and humid, so that people spent most days flocking to air-conditioned buildings or to places they could swim.

Josephine was able to put the unpleasant meeting with Michelle behind her to enjoy the most social summer she had ever known. She and Liam took full advantage of his weekends off, taking Meeghan to places of interest and accepting friends' invitations to pool parties and barbecues in both their home towns.

In August they celebrated Meeghan's fifteenth birthday.

Liam agreed to give his daughter what she had wanted and brought her to the pound to adopt a puppy. The dog of choice was a small black

Scottie, the runt of its litter. It was a male, no larger than a box of tissues, with short stubby legs and a rectangular head that appeared too large for his body. For Meeghan, it was love at first sight. She named the dog Beau.

That night after dinner, the Barnards came over to meet the newest member of the O'Dell household and to have some birthday cake. Amelia gave her best friend a new pair of blue roller-blades, and Mary McGlynn knit her an Irish cable knit sweater.

Josephine had given much thought to her gift to Meeghan. The acclaimed Celtic Dance Company was performing in Carnegie Hall, in Manhattan, and the show was receiving rave reviews in The New York Times. Tickets were virtually impossible to obtain, but Josephine used a contact name the Silvermans had given her and was able to purchase four tickets. She invited Amelia to join them.

On the night of the performance they returned home late from Manhattan with the prearranged plan to have Amelia spend the night. Meeghan kissed her father goodnight and thanked Josephine for the best night of her life before taking Amelia up to her room where they would stay up half the night chatting about the performance.

Liam and Josephine had their own sleepover planned, but Beau's need to be let out took precedence. Liam quickly took the dog outdoors before hurrying him back inside and securing him in his crate. He took the stairs two at a time, entering the bedroom to find it illuminated with candlelight and Josephine waiting for him in his bed.

This was the moment each of them had been thinking about and looking forward to for so long; but suddenly, the thought of being intimate pushed a panic button in Josephine. Even now, as Liam undressed and slid naked into bed beside her, she wondered if she was doing the right thing.

He kicked back the sheet, saying he wanted nothing between them but air, as he looked at her body for the first time. His gaze was full of longing; he filled his senses with the vision and the scent of her. Gently, Liam pulled Josephine to him, and they lay holding one another until he noticed the uncertainty in her eyes and questioned it.

"Liam, you see naked women all the time. You examine them intimately..." She could not look him in the eyes. "How do you think I feel, lying here with you now? Can you understand that I don't want to be just another naked woman to you?" She felt totally vulnerable.

Liam felt his love for her catch in his throat. Her insecurity couldn't be farther from the truth of how he felt, and he wondered how best to convince her. He pulled her closer to him and raised his head to speak softly in her ear. "I want you to listen carefully to what I am about to say. What I do for a profession is a job to me, nothing more. When I look at, or touch, a woman's body—with rubber gloves on and a nurse present in the room, I might add—it is a mechanical, clinical procedure. My patients provide a living for me. In return, I help them with their health issues and deliver their babies."

He lowered his head back on the pillow, looking deeply into the eyes of the woman he loved. "But when I touch *you*...now that's a different story. My heart beats so hard, I swear it's going to jump out of my chest. When I touch these," he said, cupping a soft breast, "I can barely breathe." His hand moved lower. "And when I touch here..."

Their union was meaningful and deliberate. It came at a time when both wanted it to happen, so that in the morning they awakened in each other's arms with no regrets, no unfulfilled expectations.

Liam had purposely asked Mary to run an errand in town so that he and Josephine should now have the house to themselves. They showered together, dressed and crept downstairs, enticed by the rich aroma of freshly brewed coffee coming from kitchen. With six eggs, some cheddar cheese, diced onions and green peppers and a few slices of ham, Liam put together an omelet that even Mrs. McGlynn could not have found fault with.

Josephine was pouring their coffee and reminiscing about the night before when she spotted a black velvet box perched on top of the fruit bowl on the center aisle. She looked at Liam, who merely shrugged his shoulders and acted as though he didn't know how it had gotten there.

"I hope you like it," he said, watching as Josephine cupped the tiny square box in her hands and held it as if it was a fragile bird. She lifted the lid and a white diamond flashed its brilliance back at her. It was a two-karat, emerald-cut stone set atop a simple antique setting of platinum gold.

"Josephine, will you marry me?" Liam reached for her hand, which slid comfortably into his strong one.

"Yes, Liam, I will!" Josephine watched as he lifted the ring from the satin lining and slipped it on the fourth finger of her left hand.

They were sealing their engagement with a kiss when Liam's buzzer went off. He removed it from the pocket of his pants to glance at the message. "Talk about bad timing. I've got to call the service," he said, bestowing a last brief peck on her waiting lips. "I'm sorry."

"Go ahead, I understand. Leave the dishes; I'll wash them."

"You are the best, and I love you." He pushed through the swinging door, intent on making his call.

Josephine held her left hand up in front of her eyes, captivated by the dazzle of the stone. "I love my ring... it is perfect!" she called out after him. She pulled on a pair of rubber gloves, washed the dishes and wiped the countertop. Then she refilled her coffee before going to join Liam in the library.

The answering service had asked him to call the attending physician at the hospital regarding one of his maternity patients. He saw Josephine enter the room and motioned that he would be hanging up momentarily, but the conversation became lengthy. Josephine sat curled up in the leather chair, holding her hand out and admiring her ring at arm's length. Repeatedly her soon-to-be new last name ran through her head, as she daydreamed about a possible wedding date.

She heard Liam finish one call and immediately dial another, this time to the patient's husband. Within minutes she fell asleep. Her left hand dangled from the arm of the chair, the diamond ring on her finger shining like a spark as it caught the ray of early morning sunlight from the window up above.

When Liam finished his call, he scribbled a hasty note and placed it on the tabletop where he was sure Josephine would see it when she opened her eyes. He bent to kiss the top of her head before taking off for the hospital.

☙

It seemed to Josephine that Marsha was intent on testing her patience as they decorated for the shop's new theme, *Autumn in New England.* All morning Marsha had been undecided and ambivalent to the point that Josephine wondered how the woman would cope with the job of decorating the window once Josephine married and moved away.

"I like that big cornucopia of gourds on the floor, but we need to move it closer to the wall. That's good, leave it right there," Marsha ordered. "And let's lift that roping of dried hydrangeas and leaves so that it drapes more naturally over the bushels of apples."

Josephine moved quickly and made the changes. It annoyed her that Marsha wouldn't leave her alone to work by herself rather than talking to her as if she didn't know the first thing about design.

"You might want to tilt that scarecrow's head. No, no, to the other side. That's it," Marsha said, already looking for something else to change.

"Why are you flapping around like this today?" Josephine challenged.

"I feel the need to get everything in place before you leave me to live in the far distant hills of Waterbridge!"

"Don't be ridiculous. You know that I'll always be just a phone call away."

"How can you be so callous?" Marsha dropped her head to glare at her employee. "You've been with me for fifteen years! A phone call away isn't going to be the same as having you here."

Minna, sensing an elevation in their voices, got up and lumbered to a far corner of the shop to once again collapse, with a thud, onto the wood floor.

Ned, who was working at the front counter, watched the dog with amusement. "Ha! Will you look at that?" he said. "I do believe you two have just been dismissed."

"In my next life, I want to be that dog," Marsha said, eyeing her pet with envy before turning back to the task at hand. "I feel as though we're running behind this year, and that I should already be working on Christmas."

"We'll be fine," Josephine assured her. "I'll still be here to set up."

"I can't believe you've chosen one of the busiest times of the year to get married."

"When is it not busy in here?"

"This is true. Secretly I am really very excited you've chosen November. It will give me the chance to show off my new coat," Marsha bragged.

"Only you would be thinking of your wardrobe. I haven't had time to look for shoes to go with my dress, and I'm the bride."

"And so what are you waiting for? Let's plan to go shopping!"

Stepping over a pumpkin to reach a bushel of apples, Josephine shrugged. "I suppose."

"Why don't you sound excited? With a rock like that you should be elated! And you should feel honored that Marc and I are willing to stand up for you two...inside a church, yet."

"We appreciate that," Josephine said. "We truly do. I wish I could put a finger on what it is I'm feeling. You're right, I should be elated about getting married, but I'm not." She hopped down from the window, searching for the cup of Chi tea she had left somewhere and forgotten. Ned found it on a stool and handed it to her.

Josephine sat down on the floor of the window with her back to Ned and lowered her voice when she spoke. "Ever since the day we got engaged, when Liam had to run off to the hospital, I've had reservations." She raised her knees to her chest and wrapped her arms around them. "Those times when he gets called away and leaves me alone with Meeghan make me think that life with him isn't going to be easy."

Marsha didn't understand what her friend was driving at. "But he's a doctor; they're notorious for being called out."

"I know. It's not just that. It's his mental absence from our lives—from Meeghan's and mine." A sigh escaped her pouting lips. "Liam is not all that's on my mind. I've been having a lot of female trouble lately."

"What kind of trouble?"

"Pain, irregular menstrual cycles. Sometimes I have dizziness and backaches. It's too soon for menopause, but..."

Marsha looked at her over the rim of her eyeglasses. "What does Liam say about it?"

"I haven't said anything to him. I don't know if I can. It's personal."

"Personal? Honey, you're about to marry the guy! This is his field of expertise. What's the matter with you?"

"Forget I mentioned it. I'll look into it after the wedding," Josephine snapped.

"I suggest you look into it sooner than that, if you want to enjoy your honeymoon."

Josephine dismissed the conversation by rising up from where she sat and, like Minna, leaving to find some other corner of the shop where she could be alone.

## CHAPTER *Nine*

Meeghan finished reading the chosen passage on marriage and, stepping down from the pulpit, smiled at her father and the woman now officially her stepmother. She took her place beside Marsha, who placed a protective arm around her and gave her a hug. They wore identical versions of the same classic silk dress, with Marsha wearing taupe and Meeghan, peach.

There, in St. Michael's Roman Catholic Church, before God and an intimate gathering of friends and relatives, Liam Thomas O'Dell and Josephine Lenore Mitchell vowed to love, honor, and obey, in sickness and in health, until death.

Josephine was a vision in a long-sleeved antique ivory lace dress with a high collar. The dress was fitted to the hips and fell to her ankles in soft folds. Her honey blond hair had been combed back and softly gathered in a chignon and accented by a single champagne rose. She carried another three in her hands to represent herself, Liam and Meeghan.

Liam's stalwart good looks were only enhanced by his dark three-piece gray wool suit, ivory shirt, and striped tie. Together he and his bride joined hands to receive the sacrament and the priest's blessing.

As she stood beside her husband, Josephine was taken back to another church, years before, when she had taken these same vows with Anthony—vows that had been selfishly broken before they saw their seventh wedding anniversary. The divorce had left her feeling afraid to love again, afraid to trust... until now. She looked down at the shining gold wedding band she had slid on Liam's finger only minutes before, and she held on to her husband's hand with the firm belief that this marriage would be a long and lasting one.

The Silvermans' home had been magically transformed for the reception. A storage company, hired to remove the furniture from their living and great rooms, had cleared enough space to accommodate fifty ivory damask cushioned chairs and five round tables draped in matching tablecloths. There were seasonal floral arrangements everywhere: exquisite sprays of sunflowers, enormous baskets of gourds, chrysanthemums and autumn leaves adding to the serenity of the room where guests could wander in and out to enjoy the music provided by a trio of musicians.

To see the details of their reception unfolding so perfectly, one would never know that Liam and Josephine had disagreed about the family pets and where they belonged on the day of the wedding. Liam believed an important occasion did not warrant the presence of anything walking on four legs, whereas Josephine argued for an animal's rightful place in the household. In the end she won out, convincing Liam he had more important things to think about and handing him a handwritted list, which included having the dogs groomed.

On the day of the wedding, Minna and Beau could be found bathed, brushed and bowed with ivory satin ribbons around their necks, hiding in the kitchen, too embarrassed to be seen.

Only Sundae was wise enough to stay out of sight, refusing to wear an ivory bow, or to have any part in the festivities. She lay under the bed upstairs patiently waiting for the household to return to normalcy.

One hour into the reception the dogs' hideaway was discovered by Josephine's nephew, Robby, who rolled with them on the floor and created a ruckus loud enough for his mother to hear.

Alex entered the kitchen and reached for her son among the frolicking canines. "Now look at you! You're all undone," she complained, bending down to tuck her son's shirt inside his pants.

"But the dogs are lonesome, Mom," Robby whined.

"Yes, but you need to stay where I can see you."

Robby raised a dimpled hand and waved a remorseful goodbye. The dogs sat panting, their eyes devotedly fixed on him until he was out of sight. Only then did they trot in unison to the corner of the kitchen where they shared a water bowl.

In the great room two young bartenders were serving drinks. A fire burned brightly in the fieldstone fireplace. Liam, who had made sure to stock Patrick McGlynn's favorite imported beer, was not surprised to see the old man be the first guest to step up to the bar. Patrick had no sooner been served when his wife appeared, pulling her husband by the sleeve of his suit jacket and escorting him to the other end of the room.

The food for the reception was an undeniable success thanks to the most sought-after caterer in the area. Five culinary staff members circulated throughout the spacious rooms, holding silver trays of hot and cold hors d'oeuvres.

A three-tier wedding cake stood in one corner of the room, its delectable spice layers separated by a whipped cream, cinnamon-flavored icing, which had been applied in soft-peaked petals. Each tier had a crowning of white chocolate shavings.

When dinner was announced, guests found their designated seats according to place cards and sat, chatting noisily, until Marc stood at the head table, tapping a crystal water goblet with the tip of his silver knife to claim their attention. He raised his glass of champagne in marked tradition, which everyone imitated.

"My wife, Marsha, and I want to welcome you to our home to honor our friends, Liam and Josephine. For those of you who do not know this, Liam and I have been friends since childhood. We grew up together on a small neighborhood street in Scarsdale. We have seen each other through trial and tribulation. Liam was my Best Man at our wedding, and I am honored today to be his." He paused to place his free hand on his wife's shoulder.

"Perhaps not as long a time, but nevertheless for years now, we have been privileged to be considered close friends of Josephine. We believe she is the perfect choice for Liam, here, since she is the only one who could take being married to someone as self-centered and egotistical as he is." Everyone laughed, some applauded. "We all are familiar with the old saying, 'Behind every man, there is a woman who....' Well, Marsha and I have no doubt that Josie Mitchell—excuse me, Josephine *O'Dell*—is going to be the driving force behind this doctor's greatness; and that together, both of them will accomplish much and know many blessings." Marc lifted his glass in the air. There was a moment's silence as glasses were raised and champagne tasted in honor of the bride and groom before the room broke into a warm, lengthy round of applause.

Meeghan wore a sentimental smile for her father and his new wife. She was rosy-cheeked and feeling quite adult with her glass of champagne. Beside her, Amelia was stone-faced, her thin white hands folded stiffly in her lap, as she waited to be ushered to the buffet table.

With their plates filled to brimming, guests resumed their conversations. To Alexandra's right sat Laura Barnard.

"Look at them," Laura said, motioning toward the newlyweds, "they are meant to be."

"They do appear to be very happy," Alex agreed, sipping her champagne. "I can't speak for Liam, but Josie deserves this. She has waited a long time to find happiness again." Smiling broadly, she caught her sister's attention across the room and waved to her. "I hope Liam knows what a lucky man he is."

Robby, who was seated between his parents, displayed youthful boredom with the conversation taking place above his head. With his plate of food virtually untouched, he slid from his chair and left the table unnoticed. He headed for the kitchen to reunite with his four-legged friends, thankful for someone to play with.

Later that night in the privacy of their bedroom, Liam and Josephine held each other through the night, reliving the memory of a wonderful day and making love into the wee hours of the morning. They awakened bright and early to rush for the airport—sleep-deprived, yet energized and excited to begin their honeymoon together as man and wife.

A commercial airline would be flying them into Dutch St. Maarten, in the West Indies; once there, they would board a small commuter plane to the island of St. Bart.

Liam had rented a white stucco villa with a terra cotta tile roof built on a cliff overlooking the sea. Breakfasts were enjoyed under the shade of a balcony veranda which extended out from their bedroom. While they basked in what appeared to be paradise, they feasted on hot buttery croissants and fluffy omelets served with sliced pineapple, mango, and papaya. There was also a small pitcher of freshly squeezed guava juice each morning and a pot of strong French coffee served with a mug of heavy cream. Like tiny beggars and thieves, tropical island birds would land on the guardrail in search of crumbs, flailing their thanks with beating wings. From the great bushes of purple allamanda and the blue petrea, their waiting mates could be heard beckoning them back to their nests.

The warm balmy days were spent sunning on some of St. Bart's famous beaches, each known for their gleaming white sands which stretched for miles along a turquoise ocean. Marigot and Lorient were secluded and quiet. But one day the beach at Petite Cul de Sac made the bride and groom feel as if it belonged to them alone. With not another soul in sight, as well as some encouragement from her husband, Josephine was able to shed her inhibition, along with her bikini top and experience the permitted topless swimming.

Liam was awestruck as he watched his wife, her mischievous laughter ringing out as she tried to keep her balance amidst the foaming sea that swirled around her hips. She reminded him of a mermaid, with her hair slicked back on her head, and her naked torso shiny wet and glistening. He remained rooted on the beach, never wanting the moment to end. He captured a picture of her in his mind, where he could recall it from the album forever kept in his heart.

In the afternoons they drove an island jeep to town, intrigued to find knotty cotton plants which grew wild along the narrow, winding road. Fluffy white puffs were stark white atop dark prickly stems, tempting tourists to pluck them if they dare. They stopped to browse in little French boutiques and market square vendors in Gustavia. It was here they bought a string of hand-painted ceramic beads and a hand-carved pipe for the McGlynns, and a silk sarong and straw hat for Meeghan. A pair of small native dolls caught Josephine's eye. They were dressed in island clothes and wearing flowers in their hair. Before leaving town, she purchased one each for Laura and Amelia.

One night they shared a tantalizing candlelight dinner and then went for a walk. They stopped for a nightcap at *Le Select*, a popular pub among the natives where sailors and locals congregate and share stories while enjoying a tropical cocktail or a cold beer. Earlier that day Josephine had begun to pale beneath her tan. She developed stomach cramps at the pub and, by the time she and Liam returned to their villa, her condition had escalated into severe pain accompanied by a low-grade fever. The pain did not dissipate until the next day and the low-grade temperature stayed with her for the remainder of their vacation.

Their honeymoon ended just as the holiday season began. As a family, the three celebrated Thanksgiving with Josephine's family in Cape Cod. Meeghan remained there for two days while her parents drove on to Clapton for a weekend with Marsha and Marc and made arrangements to ship to Waterbridge any of Josephine's belongings that hadn't already been sold.

The women went Christmas shopping while the men played their last game of golf for the season. In the evenings the four of them dined out while reminiscing about the wedding and honeymoon trip. The pace of the past two months had their effect on Josephine. It had been two weeks since their honeymoon trip, yet she was still displaying faint circles under her eyes and not feeling up to par.

Christmas arrived cold and gray, with a sprinkling of frost and the promise of snow. Liam woke early and let the women sleep in. Like a Christmas elf, he crept downstairs to take the dog outdoors and feed the pets.

He filled a small pitcher of eggnog and took it, with three cups and a plate of Christmas cookies, to the great room, where he removed a box of matches from a drawer and stooped to ignite the stack of logs Patrick had set ready in the fireplace. Flames crackled and sputtered as the dried wood caught. The fire bit into the parched crevices, causing the logs to spit forth tiny sparks, like minute firecrackers, before losing their heat and falling into the existing bed of whitened ash.

Liam and the pets congregated beside the fire, finding their favorite places and settling down. No sooner had they gotten situated, when the silence was broken by Josephine and Meeghan entering the room to bestow tender kisses and begin the long-awaited opening of presents.

Josephine sat curled up in her favorite armchair, one of the pieces from her apartment that Liam had made a place for in this room where they shared family time. She held a camera on her lap and felt sentimental at the thought of photographing their first Christmas together. Huddled beneath a cozy fleece throw, she sipped a cup of creamy eggnog while peering like stalking paparazzi through the camera lens.

Liam sat cross-legged on the floor in his flannel pajamas and doled out the presents from under the tree. Meeghan lay on her stomach beside him, her elbows on the floor and her chin resting on the palms of her hands. Her knees were bent and her feet swung freely in the air to the beat of the Christmas carols playing on the stereo. Josephine lifted the camera to her eye and, peering through the aperture, focused and pushed the button. The flash lit the room for a split second; her unsuspecting subjects moaning at being candidly captured on film.

The smell of fresh pine from the Christmas tree permeated the room while the bulbs enchanted her with an abundance of tiny colors that winked from secret hollows within the tree's outstretched branches.

The ornaments were a combination of her own treasured collection and Liam and Meeghan's accumulation over the years. One of Josephine's antique hand-blown glass balls hung next to a comic-looking ornament made of Popsicle sticks and glitter, which Meeghan had crafted as a child. The two ornaments sharing the same branch appeared a bit absurd, but both were tokens of memories past, and Josephine would not separate them.

Marsha and Marc were expected by noon, and Josephine began to feel the pressure of having to prepare dinner. The McGlynns were away for the holiday, and she had been up late the night before making the stuffing for the Christmas goose and preparing what she could ahead of time. The opening of gifts had taken longer than expected, and in her head she could hear Mary's firm instruction to get the bird in the oven on time. At least she had thought to set the dining table the night before. Putting her camera aside, she rose from her reverie to follow the mental telepathy of an absent cook.

Liam and Meeghan were left sitting among clouds of wrinkled tissue paper and stacks of boxes, tangled in tails of red and green ribbon which hung like trophies around their necks. Beau and Sundae dozed contentedly nearby, hypnotized by the glowing embers that sedated them with their unyielding heat.

This was Josephine's little family that she loved so much and was so very grateful for. Alone in the kitchen she offered thanks for the birth of Jesus Christ, as well as for her own rebirth, for she truly felt reborn since marrying Liam and inadvertently inheriting a daughter.

Outside a squall blew about haphazardly in the blustering wind. The snow was already beginning to stick to the ground in a wet dusting that covered the ground and the trees in a blanket of white. The forecast had predicted a deep accumulation. Josephine pressed the tip of her nose against the cold glass of the kitchen window and thrilled, with childlike wonder, to the sight of a traditional white Christmas.

The timer on the stove began to buzz shrilly, reminding her that the potatoes needed peeling and the mushroom caps still hadn't been stuffed.

CR

# CHAPTER *Ten*

"It says here you've been experiencing an unusual amount of abdominal pain and that your legs have been giving you some problems?" Doctor Ira Goldstein lowered the chart to peer at the new patient lying flat on the examining table. He felt the pressure of knowing that, not only was this his boss's wife, but that there could be something very wrong with her.

"Yes, that is correct," Josephine answered.

"When was your last pap?"

"About a year ago."

"I see. All right then. I'd like to do a pelvic and breast exam on you now. We'll take a look at your pap results and go from there."

When he had finished examining her, Dr. Goldstein asked Josephine to dress and then join him in his office. Behind closed doors he said, "Offhand, I don't see anything to worry about. However, I'll have to see the results of the pap before we can say for sure." He scribbled illegibly across a prescription pad. "I'm ordering some blood work, and I'd like you to see a specialist, a gastroenterologist. We can refer you to one, if you like." He saw his patient's eyebrows lift with concern. "It's just precautionary. I'm sure Liam would agree you should be looked at. That way we cover all bases."

"I suppose."

"All right then. I'll ask Liam, but I believe the doctor he will want you to see is Saul Lieberman. He's excellent."

"I'll call Doctor Lieberman, but I prefer you not discuss this with Liam. He has so much on his mind, and I don't wish to worry him unnecessarily."

"I understand, but you need to know that should Liam approach me about your tests..."

"I'll tell Liam myself. Do the best you can for me, please?"

Ira handed Josephine the scripts and rose to shake her hand. "You'll get the usual form letter in the mail when your pap results come in. And it goes without saying that I will call you personally if there is any reason for concern."

Josephine relaxed under his smile; his self-assurance was encouraging. "Thanks, Ira. This is one time I can say I hope we won't have to see each other for a while."

Two weeks later she followed through with a scheduled appointment with Dr. Lieberman who reviewed her file and recommended a blood draw, a pelvic sonogram, and a barium test.

When all three test results came back negative, Saul Lieberman diagnosed her condition as being stress-related. He suspected the wedding and the relocation to a new area had taken its toll on her system. He prescribed a medication for anxiety along with an antacid and told her to check in with him again in three months.

The shadow of a doubt lay dormant beneath her heart as Saul Lieberman delivered his diagnosis. But since his opinion was what she wanted to believe, Josephine left his office without making a follow-up appointment. Like an ostrich, she was burying her head in the sand.

A class of twenty-five students listened as their Celtic dance instructor, Denis O'Shea, reviewed the anticipated goals inside the Dream Catcher Dance Studio in downtown Manhattan.

Meeghan, dressed in black tights, a T-shirt, and dance slippers, sat cross-legged on the floor. She and the other students listened and observed in rapt attention as their teacher told them what they could accomplish if they worked hard.

Denis O'Shea was charismatic, and his students looked on him as if he were a god. When he demonstrated for them, putting his instructions to music in the form of synchronized body movement, there were gasps and tear-filled eyes for the sheer beauty of his portrayal of this ancient form of art.

Denis was tall, lean and muscular, with the grace and balance of a professional dancer. He slowly paced back and forth before the group, his voice carrying to every corner of the large studio. He studied their faces as he spoke to them. Their expressions, posture and overall body language revealed volumes to him. Within minutes he could identify those who were destined to excel as well as those who would quit within a month's time.

"Everything we do here is accelerated to the nth degree," he told them. "Some of you will barely be able to walk after the first few lessons; others of you will leave here crying or, better yet, you'll quit. That's good." He paused to savor the group's reaction to his remark. "Why is it good, you wonder? Because I would rather you quit early on than to waste my time and the time of students who carry the love of this dance in their blood." He let his words take effect before continuing. "The injury rate here is high. In order to maintain precision, we must constantly drill. We must practice long hours, often without taking a break. We'll do a routine over and over until we get it right, and I will not care how long that takes. I don't care about your homework. I don't care about your parents. I don't care if you are vomiting from exertion. What I do care about is this dance. And I care about this company. But most of all, I care about my heritage. And that is why, ladies and gentlemen, I will be relentless with you."

He stopped to take a swig from a water bottle. "There will be pain. It's there all the time. It won't always be physical pain. Sometimes it will be emotional pain, or spiritual pain. But I will teach you how to embrace that pain—how to work with it to an advantage. Every lesson will be harder than the one before it. Are there any questions?"

He eyed the group warily. Each student was riveted to the spot where they sat or stood. If any of them had any questions, they were afraid to ask them. Even the parents who sat in a room adjacent to the dance studio and who had heard the instructor's speech were silent, ready to write out their tuition checks to this persuasive man.

"All right, then," Denis called out. "Let's dance!"

Mrs. McGlynn had set the table and laid out a cold supper according to the new Thursday night routine. Josephine and Meeghan rode the train back to the Waterbridge station where they had left a car in the commuter parking lot.

They were no sooner home when Meeghan showered and lay down to rest. When she slept through the call for supper, Liam asked, "Don't you think this is too stringent a schedule for her? I don't like her starting her homework so late. I'm concerned about her grades falling." He stabbed a slice of pork served from the platter his wife held for him.

"I have never seen her happier than she was today in that classroom." Josephine nibbled at a breadstick before placing it on her plate with the rest of her unfinished meal. "And have you noticed how trim she's getting? She's stopped biting her nails, too. You can't deny Meggie has worked long and hard for this."

"Yes, she has," Liam agreed. "She's looking very well. How did you feel she did in the class? Did the instructor try them out? Is she any good?"

"He had them try a little choreographed routine. Mr. O'Shea feels Meggie is a natural. He told me that with discipline she may well become one of the best dancers in the troupe."

Liam was surprised. "No kidding. So then these lessons will be worth the big check I'm writing every month?"

"Yes," Josephine smirked, tapping her husband on his arm. "Meggie's happiness *alone* is worth writing the check for. Wait till you see the recital at the end of the year. You're not going to believe how good she will be by then."

"She has you to thank for these lessons. I hope she realizes that."

"I'm the one who is thankful. I wish you could have seen us, Liam. We had such a good time riding down on the train. We talked and shared. You know, sometimes we disagree about certain things, but that's to be expected and it's not very often. And when we do disagree, we make up soon afterwards. We're never on the outs for long. I guess that's because Meeghan knows that down deep, the love is there."

Liam looked at his wife and saw her affection for him softly mirrored in her eyes.

Josephine smiled. "I wouldn't trade this time for *anything*, and I thank you for making it possible for Meggie to go."

"Speaking of going, why haven't you made that follow up appointment with Lieberman like you were supposed to do three months ago?"

"Because."

"Because, why?"

"I don't know," Josephine shrugged. "Neither Doctor Lieberman nor Ira found anything wrong. What's the point of a follow up visit?"

"The point is that you're still having symptomatic pain. I want to find out what this is all about. I wish you'd let me run some tests."

"I'll go eventually. I promise. Right now I'm into Meggie and the dance thing. I enjoy taking her where she needs to go. I don't know that I have any time for myself right now."

"Don't make excuses, Josie, you're procrastinating and you know it."

"I'll go, I'll go," she said, rolling her eyes. "Pass me the potatoes, will you, please?"

"Here, take plenty," Liam urged, handing her the bowl. "You look as though you need to put on a few pounds."

"I'm fine. There's not been much time for me to eat lately, that's all. Laura's keeping me busy with the garden club, too. This is the beginning of our busy season, and the women's guild at church has asked me to help with this year's fund raiser." She heaped a scoop of potatoes onto her plate in an effort to divert his attention from her noticeable weight loss.

"I don't like it," Liam frowned.

"What don't you like?"

"The recurring fevers, the leg cramps. I want to talk to Ira about running some other tests."

"I think you ought to mind your business and let me take care of myself. I'm a big girl."

"Yes, but you're not a doctor..."

"And you're not *my* doctor." The remark sounded harsher than she had meant it to. She saw that she had offended him and quickly tried to explain. "It's just that if Ira didn't work for you, you'd not be privy to any more than I'd want you to know."

"I should think that as my wife, you would want to tell me everything."

"I do," Josephine soothed, noting the irritation in his voice. "But having you discuss my health with Ira makes me feel as though you are my parent, rather than my husband."

"And your procrastination about seeking medical attention has me feeling like you are my child, rather than my wife!" Liam removed his napkin from his lap, and pushed his chair from the table. "I'll be in the library. I've got some work to do."

He had no sooner left the room than Mary entered through the swinging door and began removing the dishes. It was obvious by her solemn expression that she had overheard their argument.

"Will you be having dessert, Ma'am? I've made a fine peach torte."

"Thank you, no, Mary." Not wanting to disappoint the woman, she added, "I'd appreciate your putting it out for lunch tomorrow, though. And please take some home tonight for yourself and your husband."

"Patrick will appreciate that."

"Be sure to leave a dinner plate for Meggie, will you? I'm going upstairs now to wake her."

"I've got it all set aside. My, but the child has surely slimmed down."

Josephine remained at the table alone with her thoughts. She was tired and longed to go to bed, but she needed to wake Meggie for supper, and someone had to stay up long enough to make sure she completed her homework.

She lifted a hand to her forehead and confirmed another rise in her temperature. It was important she get to bed if she had any hope of joining her garden club the next day to plant geraniums in the barrels in front of all the village storefronts.

Feeling he was not alone in the library, Liam looked up to find his wife standing in the doorway. "Yes? What is it?"

"I need to go to bed. I'll wake Meggie, but will you sit with her so she won't have to eat her supper alone?"

"Yes."

"Good. I'm sure she will want to tell you about the auditions. And will you see that she gets her homework done?"

"I think I can manage that."

"I'll see you upstairs then. Good night." She waited for his response. When it didn't come, she turned and walked away. Her feet felt leaden as she shuffled towards the staircase.

Liam watched her turn and leave. Had she been more agreeable at dinner, he would have been more considerate. But she had been defiant, and his darker side was not sorry now to see her hurting. The image of her heading toward the stairs, her shoulders slumped in defeat, would one day haunt his dreams. But tonight, with a heart of stone, he watched her go and was only too glad for some peace and quiet.

"I've woken you?" Laura Bernard asked incredulously. "We're going to be late, Josie."

"I don't think I can garden today, Laura. I'm sorry. I put in a pretty bad night."

"Are you sick? What's wrong?"

"I don't know. I think I've pinched a nerve in my lower back or something. My legs have been giving me a lot of trouble lately. I don't think I should be bending over the barrels today. Are you short of help?"

"No, no. I'm sure there will be a good turnout. It's such a beautiful day. I'm sorry you can't be with us. Can I bring you anything from town?"

"I'll be fine. Mary and Patrick are here if I need anything."

"I've got some news to share. I had planned to tell you on the way over this morning, but now you aren't coming. What if I stop by when I'm done planting?"

"Sure, that would be fine. Is it good news, or bad?"

"Good. It's a surprise," Laura said, heightening the suspense. "I'll see you after lunch."

At two o'clock, Laura's arrival was marked by Beau, who was at the door barking before she had a chance to ring the doorbell.

Josephine greeted her neighbor warmly and brought her into the kitchen. Both were aware they had less than an hour before their children were home from school; they needed to make the most of this time alone.

Beau was left behind as the two women moved outdoors to sit beside the pool with glasses of iced tea. His curly head hung low, and his two jet black eyes watched woefully as he was ignored.

"I can't believe you've got your pool opened this early," Laura said. "David doesn't open ours before Memorial Day."

"I know. Crazy, isn't it? Would you believe Liam and Meggie have been swimming already?" Josephine said, shaking her head in mock disbelief. "Even though it's heated, you wouldn't catch me in there this time of year!" The thought caused her to involuntarily wrap the sides of her sweater closer to her body.

"You look better than you sounded this morning," Laura lied. She thought her friend looked pale. "How are you feeling?"

"Better, thanks. I'm sorry to have let you down this morning. I had honestly been looking forward to going."

"We made out fine, but you were missed. All the girls asked for you. The barrels look good, though. We planted pink geraniums. Now it will be up to the store owners to water and dead-head them and keep their barrels watered. Most of them are good about it, but we still have to remind some of them from time to time."

They sipped iced teas while Josephine waited for Laura to say what she had come to tell her.

"David and I have some wonderful news," Laura said, nervously smoothing the fabric of her slacks with her fingers. "We've met with a specialist in Manhattan, an ophthalmologist. He examined Amelia and feels she is, at her age, an excellent candidate for a prosthetic eye. He wants her to have the surgery at the end of the school year."

"Oh, Laura, that's wonderful! Josephine moved her chair closer and took hold of her friend's hand. "How does Amelia feel about it?"

"Apprehensive. Frightened. But overall, she's thrilled. The doctor assures us he can provide a perfect match."

"Amelia has such outstanding eye color. Her good looks can only be enhanced by this surgery. You must promise to let us help in whatever way we can. Meggie, too, will want to be there for her."

"Thanks, Josie. Mother will come out to stay with the twins, but David and I will feel better knowing you're here in case she needs anything while we're at the hospital. Please promise not to mention this to Meggie. I know Amelia would want to tell her herself."

"Of course."

"I can't begin to tell you what this means to us." Laura began to cry at the thought of the surgery's anticipated success, coupled with fear of possible complication.

Josephine rose from her chair and raised her friend out of her seat. She enfolded Laura into a warm embrace while she stroked her back, gently assuring her that the surgery was going to go fine. Laura wiped her eyes with her fingertips, laying her head on Josephine's shoulder. In hushed tones, they spoke of their friendship while holding fast to one another and the impending dream come true.

ᏣᏋ

# CHAPTER *Eleven*

The twins' laughter could be heard through the bedroom door as David Barnard carried the large present up the stairs with Josephine following behind him. "How are you feeling?" he asked her. "Laura tells me you've been having some health issues."

"I'm not sure what symptoms are real, or just my imagination. Liam's office is running tests. But I feel pretty good today."

"That's good. We can't have the new bride sick, now can we?"

"I hardly feel like a new bride anymore," Josephine laughed.

Behind the door the twins were becoming too rowdy for their father's liking. David grimaced. "Ah, summer vacation! Laura and I can barely wait for school to start. I've got the box, if you will just give a knock," David said, trying to maneuver his large frame and the present within the confines of the hallway.

Josephine rapped on the door, and the voices behind it immediately fell silent. Some shuffling and a bark from Huckleberry preceded Amelia's voice permitting them to enter.

"Honey, Mrs. O'Dell has come to see you," David said, handing his daughter the tall box wrapped in purple paper and tied with a wide bright pink ribbon.

Huckleberry bounded from across the room to welcome Josephine with several sloppy licks of his tongue, but Jeremy pushed the dog aside in his rush to assess the box. "Wow! Look at the size of that!"

"It's almost as tall as we are!" Scott declared, situating himself on the bed beside his sister.

"Hello, boys," Josephine greeted, affectionately rubbing two shaggy heads. "Hello, Amelia. I hope I've not come at a bad time."

"No, it's fine." Amelia, feeling conspicuous, looked every bit the pirate with a white patch over one eye.

"I've brought some presents." Josephine reached into the shopping bag she held and brought out two small wrapped packages. She handed one to each of the twins.

"Gee, thanks, Mrs. O'Dell," Scott said.

"Yes, thank you, for whatever it is," Jeremy agreed, tearing off the wrapping. "Oh, wow! This is so great!" he cried, holding up a video starring his favorite super hero.

"And look!" Scott echoed. He held his own movie before his brother's face. "It's the one we wanted!"

The twins begged their father to let them view them, even though the weather warranted their playing outdoors. David reminded them to remember their manners; and after bestowing a kiss of thanks on Josephine's cheek, the twins tumbled from their sister's room to race each other down the stairs.

"Don't run!" David yelled after them, but his order fell on deaf ears. "I'd better get down there. Those hooligans are liable to break the TV. Thanks for the gifts." He gave Josephine a peck on the cheek and left the room, but not before shooting a warning glance in his daughter's direction.

"Meeghan told me you have a hundred champion ribbons hanging in your room. It looks to me like there could be more than that," Josephine said, trying to start a conversation.

"Why didn't Meggie come with you?"

"She's babysitting. But she told me to tell you she will call you later when she gets home." Unease hung around them like a heavy cloak. "You've got a great room here. I like your posters. Thanks to Meggie, I bet I could name some of these rock stars." The small talk didn't seem to be working, so Josephine got to the point. "So how are you feeling?"

"Pretty good, I guess. The eye feels weird, though."

"I'm sure it does, but you will soon adjust to it."

"That's what the doctor says. He told me that it won't be long before I won't even think about it."

"I'm sure he's correct," Josephine reassured. "Would you like to open your present now?"

"Okay."

She held the box while Amelia slid the large satin ribbon off it and lifted the top. Under several sheets of tissue paper, she uncovered a three-foot antique porcelain doll dressed in black riding breeches, a red jacket and black leather riding boots. Beneath a black velvet riding cap, the doll's curly golden hair was gathered in a pony tail, and her hand-painted pink lips were shiny and beautifully sculpted. Their corners turned upward in a coquettish smile, as if the doll was keeping a secret.

But its pale blue eyes were the main reason Josephine had bought the doll. They were magnificent in their glassy splendor. Deep and crystal clear, they were perfectly positioned beneath long brown curling lashes and, like Amelia's, had multi-faceted irises that resembled two ice blue diamonds.

"Oh!" gasped Amelia. "She is beautiful!"

"She is," Josephine agreed, "but she will need a name."

Amelia hesitated but a moment. "January!" she said. "I want to name her January."

"That's an unusual name."

"I was born in that month. I've always loved the sound of it." She held the doll in her arms as if it were a bouquet of flowers. "Where did you get her?"

"I started looking for her as soon as your mother told me you were having surgery. I knew right away I wanted to find a doll with eyes as beautiful as yours. I did a lot of research on line. When I found this one, dressed in that outfit, I knew she was the one."

Amelia looked up at Josephine with a singular blue eye. Her lip trembled. "I haven't told my parents, but I really want to ride again."

"I see. And what do you think your parents will have to say about that?"

"They'll forbid it."

"But you won't know unless you ask them, right?"

"I'm frightened," Amelia whispered.

"Don't be. Your parents love you. I'm sure they want to see you fulfill all your dreams." She hesitated, not wanting to mislead the child into believing her parents would permit her to ride again if that were not the case. "Perhaps when you are feeling stronger, you might talk to your mom and dad about it."

"They'll never allow it, I'm sure of it."

"You can't be sure of anything until you try asking for it." Josephine covered the young girl's hand with her own. "How about writing a list for your parents telling them all the reasons you wish to resume riding lessons?"

"I could think of a million."

"Good. So now you've got something important to work on while you recuperate."

"You won't say anything to mom, will you?"

"It's not my place to do that. It's for you to discuss with your parents when you feel ready. I promise not even to tell Meeghan."

"Oh, I don't mind if Meggie knows; she's my best friend."

"And you are Meggie's. Still, I think you should be the one to tell her."

"Okay." Amelia pulled the doll to her face and placed her soft warm cheek against the cold porcelain one. "I love January!"

"Are you referring to the month, or the doll?"

"Both." Amelia hesitated for a few seconds and then gathered her courage. "I know I haven't been very nice to you in the past. I guess I was wrong; Meggie is very lucky to have you for a mom."

"I'm lucky to have her for a daughter. And as for you and me," Josephine said, touched by the child's apology, "what do you say we start all over?"

"It's a deal."

"All right then. But for now, I am going to leave so that you can rest and think about some of those reasons you've got to come up with for your parents."

Rising from the bed, Josephine bent over and placed a gentle kiss atop the child's head. As she turned to leave, Amelia grabbed her hand. "Wait! Don't you want to see my new eye?"

Josephine was caught off guard. "Are you supposed to be removing the patch?"

"Yes. Actually, I have certain times of the day when I'm not supposed to wear it." Amelia gently lifted the white padded patch held in place by a thin elastic cord. She blinked a few times, her face contorting until she adjusted to the light and the unfamiliar feel and newness of her prosthesis. Despite the redness and the slight swelling around it, the glass eye was a perfect match in both size and color to her natural one. Her eyebrows rose in anticipation of a compliment.

Shaking her head in amazement, Josephine placed her hand over Amelia's hand with maternal tenderness. "So, do you want my honest opinion?"

"I guess."

"I may have bought the wrong doll."

"Why do you say that?"

"Because," Josephine smiled, "it looks like January's eyes are not nearly as lovely as yours!"

cR

The hospital saw to it that the wife of the Head of Obstetrics was assured a private room in the new wing that had recently been added on through the generosity of a contributing foundation.

Josephine sat up in bed staring out the large picture window that overlooked an attractive circular garden. The view from the third floor made it difficult to identify which flowers were in bloom, but she could accurately name almost all of them. Trivial a game as this was, it kept her mind off the tests she had undergone earlier in the day and kept her occupied while waiting for the results.

Twenty-four hours earlier her blood had been drawn and an ultrasound and mammogram performed, plus several x-rays taken. Next a CAT scan was taken, after which Doctor Goldstein had extracted abdominal fluid for analysis. All tests results were now being reviewed and compiled as Josephine pondered her flowers in the garden below.

She had Liam paged so he could be with her when Ira came back to report his findings. The ticking of the clock on the wall of her room coincided with the beating of her heart; the rhythmic duet making the silent waiting seem endless and all the more excruciating. Josephine laid her head back on the pillow and willed herself to relax. Minutes turned to hours until finally the colors of the garden below melted into one another as sleep took over. She had slept less than an hour when the whisperings of men's voices woke her.

"Kyoto's reputation speaks for itself, Liam. He knows what he's doing."

"I agree, but I want him to move on this. No waiting, no postponing."

"I'm sure Kyoto will not procrastinate."

"Liam," Josephine said sleepily, "you're here."

"I sure am, baby. Had a little nap, did you?"

"I guess I did." She smoothed a hand over her face and ran her fingers haphazardly through her hair. "Hello, Ira."

Ira Goldstein recognized the trepidation in his patient's eyes, and he wished at this moment it could be any other physician having to deliver this news. "Josephine," he said, clearing his throat, "we've got your results." He let the clipboard fall to his side, as he glanced first at Liam and then at his patient. Josephine suspected he had something serious to tell her; the smile with which she intended to put him at ease was weak with fear.

"Tell me, Ira, I can handle it."

"You have a malignancy, Josephine. I'm sorry."

The room was spinning. Liam was trying to hold her in his arms, but she was pushing him away.

"Where? Where is it?" She could hear her own voice sounding shrill.

"It's your ovaries. There are tumors. I am advising a hysterectomy as soon as possible."

Josephine's breathing became erratic. "Is this what you advise, Liam? What do you think?" Even in her husband's solid embrace, she shook uncontrollably.

"I think," Liam said with false resolve, "that you are in excellent hands and that we will have every expert following this all the way." He kissed the top of her head, trying to soothe her. "Ira is a superb gynecologist; I trust him implicitly. You must also. After the hysterectomy he and Kyoto Chin, the oncologist assigned to you, will work together with me to formulate your chemotherapy."

Josephine knew she was in for a bad time. "This means I'm going to lose my hair, doesn't it? I'll be sick?" She wanted to be brave, but she already felt nauseous at the thought of what she was going to be in for.

"We don't know that for sure," Liam lied. "Let's take one step at a time, okay? Just one day at a time." He looked at Ira. "I'd like to schedule the surgery for Thursday. That gives us tomorrow for prepping."

"I agree. How about it, Josie? Are you ready to fight this thing?"

Josephine didn't answer. She had buried her face in her husband's chest, willing herself to disappear. Her world was completely shattered. She forced her mind to visualize the peaceful setting of the circular garden outside, concentrating on the richness of color and fragrances she knew so well. Better to think of beauty rather than the cancer cells multiplying inside her.

Someone was calling her name, asking if she was all right, but she couldn't answer. For in her mind she saw them—the dead flowers. They lay brown and rotting on the bottom of the flowerbed in the circular garden. They were being overshadowed and outnumbered by those in full bloom, which grew on sturdy green stems and reached radiantly toward the sun.

# Two

2001

ଔ

# CHAPTER *Twelve*

"Oops! Sorry," Alex muttered, as a flustered valet sat on a squeaky rubber duck left on the front seat of her car. "Just throw that on the floor with the other stuff," she directed, as she thanked him and hurried toward the lobby of the Boston Hotel. She was more than fashionably late for her sister's luncheon.

She ran a free hand through her wavy brown hair as she made her way to the corner table in the hotel restaurant where Marsha and Ned were giving a drink order to their waiter.

"Sorry I'm late. The traffic is murderous out there today." She took a seat beside Marsha, who greeted her with a lipstick kiss that left an imprint on her tanned cheek.

"Hello, Alex. How is Josie? How long did you stay with her?"

Alex inconspicuously rubbed her thumb over the lipstick mark she couldn't see but was sure was there. "I got there the day she came home from the hospital and I stayed with her for the first week. She had a rough go of it at first. The incision gave her a lot of discomfort, but now she's doing fine. You'll see."

"We've ordered cocktails. What's your poison?" Ned asked.

"White wine, please, well-chilled."

"Excuse me. Yoo hoo!" Ned flagged the waiter. "We need another drink over here when you have a chance."

"Make that two!" Josephine appeared at the table, dressed in gray wool slacks and a black sweater with a paisley scarf tied at the shoulder.

"Josie! Hello, honey! Oh, my God! It is so good to see you!" Marsha was already out of her seat, smothering her friend in a fierce bear hug. She held her at arm's length. "Look at you! I should look so good!"

The familiar scent of Marsha's perfume was comforting to Josephine, who was once again smothered in a full-body embrace for what seemed an eternity. "Hello, Marsha. I've missed you."

Alex waited her turn. She gently kissed her sister, holding Josephine's face in both her hands. "I'm glad you'll be spending the night with me. Robby is so excited Auntie is coming."

Josephine broke away and made her way around the table to Ned, who had risen and was waiting patiently for his turn with her. "Hello, Ned." She hugged and kissed him affectionately.

"Sweetie, you are way too thin!" Ned observed. "You know Marsha doesn't like anyone whose hips are smaller than hers!"

"That's the truth," Marsha agreed.

Their laughter broke the last of the maudlin mood, and as they took their seats around the table, everyone was smiling.

Ned, who had helped seat Josephine, bent low to whisper in her ear. "The old girl has been working me like a bitch!"

"I heard that," Marsha said. "Don't you dare believe a word he says, Josephine. I swear he hasn't done a lick of work since you left."

After the waiter had taken their food orders, Marsha got right to the heart of the matter. "So? What are the doctors telling you?"

"They say I'm to begin chemotherapy soon. They've inserted a Port-A-Cath in my chest to make it easier for me to receive the treatments."

Ned paled.

"I thought you were a trooper after surgery," Alex remarked. "I could never have been as brave."

"I'm fine, just fine. Doctor Goldstein believes they got all the cancer. After my chemo treatments, he has every hope that I will be as good as new." Josephine sighed. "Now I appreciate all your concern, honestly I do. But I didn't drive all this way to get depressed. So someone change the subject, quick! I haven't had a good laugh in months!"

The waiter arrived with two orders of Caesar salad with grilled chicken for Marsha and Alex. Ned had a club sandwich with an order of fries, and Josephine had ordered a bowl of New England clam chowder and a slice of baked quiche.

Marsha told the latest stories about the shop. It surprised Josephine to learn that customers were still asking for her and that even Minna had fallen into a temporary slump after she left.

"It took Marc and me weeks to lift her out of her depression," Marsha kidded. "Like a typical female, I had to take her shopping for new bandannas and out for ice cream before she became bearable again."

"Oh, Marsha," Josephine laughed, "you're too much! This is what I've missed—all of you and all your crazy stories!"

"Pass the ketchup, will you, please?" Ned asked. "So, sweetie, how's step-motherhood?"

"It keeps me busy, but I like it. Meggie's a good kid."

"Do you think she likes you?"

"I hope so. I believe she does. We have our disagreements from time to time, but the good times far outnumber the bad."

"Now the fun begins," Marsha interjected, taking a sip of her lime margarita.

"Josie, remember how Mom treated us when we were teenagers?" Alex chuckled out loud. "I thought for a while there we were going to need Dad to tell us the facts of life!"

"I remember," Josephine said. "Mom never enjoyed talking about anything personal, especially sex!"

"Lots of mothers are like that," Ned said.

"But I'm talking about even *after* we were married!"

"We're not kidding," Alex cried. "With Mom, it was as though sex didn't exist. When I became pregnant, I swear our mother didn't understand how it could have happened! That kind of stuff about her used to drive Rob crazy."

Marsha shook her head. "Not my mother. She called every Yenta in our neighborhood when I got my first period. I was only thirteen years old, and already she was looking to find me a husband!"

Ned waved his hand in the air, volleying for attention. "Well, ladies, when Matthew and I moved in together, my mother asked if we planned on giving her any grandchildren! Talk about being clueless!"

It was small talk and chatter that made the afternoon pass all too quickly, as their laughter reverberated throughout the room until one of them noticed the time, and the luncheon swiftly came to an end. It had been a positive visit for Josephine. She was able to shelve her problems, if only for a few hours, and lose herself in the joy and comfort of those closest to her. When it came time to leave she clung to Marsha and Ned, pressing both of them to her heart as she outwardly expressed her affections.

The drive to Cape Cod was an easy one, as she followed her sister home and spent two days relaxing at the beach with Alex and her son. It was the second week in September and most of the tourists were gone. The ocean offered a vast visual retreat, where Josephine could forget her fear of cancer and gather strength from the tides that ebbed and flowed.

She missed Liam immensely, but it was Meggie she found herself longing for. The night before she left for home, she phoned her. "Hello, honeybunch!"

"Josie? Where are you?"

"I'm still at Aunt Alex's, but I'll be leaving to come home tomorrow."

"Good. I miss you."

"Oh, sweetie, you have no idea how much I miss *you*! How is everything there?"

"Fine. Mr. O'Shea is killing us, but I've learned this neat routine, and he says he may put me in the front line for the Christmas recital."

"Good for you! That's great. How's Amelia?"

"She's fine. Her patch is off for good now."

"Tell her I'll be anxious to see her." Josephine was feeling tired. "Is Dad home? Can I speak to him?"

"He called just before you did. He's on his way back from the hospital."

"When he comes in, tell him not to call me tonight. I'm feeling a little worn out. I'm going to bed soon."

"Are you okay?"

"Sure. Just sleepy, that's all, and I'll be leaving early tomorrow to come home." She avoided mentioning the fever she knew she was running.

"What time will you be here?" Meeghan asked.

"Mid-afternoon. Let Mrs. McGlynn know I'll be home for dinner, will you?"

"Sure. Till tomorrow then. I love you."

"I love you more, Meggie." The fever only added to Josephine's feeling of melancholy. The thought of the long drive back the next day was unappealing at best.

Upstairs she could hear Robby whining. He was giving his parents a hard time about putting on his pajamas and was refusing to kiss them goodnight. His favorite stuffed animal lay on the floor in front of the television. Josephine stooped to pick it up. It was a fat green frog, as large as a basketball, with large popping eyes. She squeezed its stomach: the frog's mouth opened and a long red felt tongue stuck out with a fly on the end of it.

Wearily, she tucked the frog under her arm and headed for the stairs. Her body ached for the comfort of her own bed, the manly warmth of her husband, and for the affection of their daughter, who every night dressed herself in her own pajamas, no longer left her toys on the floor, and never went to bed without kissing her parents goodnight.

# CHAPTER *Thirteen*

Yvonne, a young stylist with spiked hair and large loop ear rings peered through the window of the beauty salon. "Will you just look at that sky? It looks as though it can't make up its mind what to do."

Josephine sat in the leather chair with a black cape fastened around her neck. "The weather channel is calling for rain, but I wouldn't be surprised to see snow."

"Please," Yvonne said, "it's only September. Let's not rush the fall, it's my favorite time of year." She pumped on the metal bar at the base of the chair until it was elevated to the proper height. Removing the terrycloth towel from Josephine's head, she released a healthy amount of wet shoulder-length hair. "Tomorrow you are going to be the most chic patient in the hospital," Yvonne assured her.

"I'm afraid my *chic-ness* will not last long. The doctor tells me my hair should begin falling out after the second chemo treatment."

"You have beautiful hair. It's going to break my heart to cut it," Yvonne said, lifting a dampened lock between her fingers. "Just how short are we talking?" Her scissors were held in readiness.

"Very."

"I don't want to take too much."

"Not to worry. In less than a month there won't be a hair left on my head. Let's go for it!" Josephine surprised herself with her own resolve.

It was easy to maintain a sense of humor when reality had not yet set in.

Thick clumps of wet hair fell to the linoleum floor like dead snakes. Yvonne's fingers moved deftly and with a swiftness that left no time for change of mind, much less regret. Twenty minutes later a stunned Josephine stood looking at her reflection in the mirror. Her hair was no more than two inches long all over her head.

Yvonne rubbed some styling gel into her palms and ran it through what remained of her client's hair, pulling it through until it spiked outward. "How do you like it?"

"I feel like a porcupine, but it's exactly what I had in mind." Already she was sorry.

"That's why I used the styling gel. It gives volume to the cut. We sell it here, if you'd like to have some to use at home."

"I'm fairly sure I won't have any use for it. Thanks anyway, Yvonne."

The young girl reddened. "I'm sorry, I forgot."

"No problem. How much do I owe you?" Josephine asked, looking out at the smoldering sky and noticing that a heavy wind had kicked up while she had been in the chair. She was anxious to get home.

"There's no charge."

"What? No, no, I — "

"Please, Josephine. I'd like to do this for you, if you don't mind."

Josephine acquiesced. "This is uncomfortable for me, but thank you. However, I insist on leaving a tip."

"I wish you wouldn't."

But the folded bill had already been tucked under the pair of shiny scissors at the cutter's station.

"Thank you, Yvonne. This was very kind of you."

"Goodbye, Josephine. Good luck. Come back soon."

"As soon as I have my hair back, I will." She smiled wryly and walked out of the salon.

The gusts of wind blew across her head, forcing her to lift the collar of her raincoat to cover her ears, which now were exposed to the elements. With her skirt whipping around her legs, she reached her car, jumped into the driver's seat, and quickly slammed the door.

The trees bent their heavy limbs in surrender to the wind, sending their turning leaves to scatter while an ominous, massive black cloud hovered high above the county.

Back inside the salon, Yvonne had been sweeping Josephine's hair clippings into a dustpan. As she carefully dumped them into a metal trash can, an inner sadness swept over her, and she was suddenly met with an irresistible urge to hear her mother's voice. She made a mental note to call her when she got off work. Absently she removed the folded bill from under the pair of scissors. She was about to slip it into her pocket with the rest of her tips when she noticed the face of President Ulysses S. Grant staring back at her. Josephine O'Dell had left her a fifty-dollar tip.

In Manhattan, on the corner of Forty-Sixth and Broadway, Meeghan stood waiting for her ride home from dance class. It had been an invigorating workout and the teacher was especially pleased with her performance. "Aye, you've come a long way, Meggie," Denis O'Shea had told her, "from the awkward girl you were when first we met!"

Her dance partner, Bruce Spantelli, stood beside her on their usual spot outside the steps of the studio. His family lived on the Upper West Side. Bruce had an Italian father, who wished he would help out with the family's canning business after school, and an Irish mother who encouraged her son to dance.

Waiting with Meeghan until her ride arrived was never an imposition to Bruce. In truth, he had a crush on her, but he was too shy to let her know it, and Meeghan was too wrapped up in herself to recognize his feelings. Still, she adored Bruce and thought of him as a perfect dance partner as well as a good friend. Although neither of them had a moment to spare during class—for Mr. O'Shea would dismiss from the company any student he found slacking off during practice—they looked forward to spending time together while Meeghan waited for her ride home.

Sometimes, when they knew her ride would be late, Meeghan and Bruce would walk across the street to the Italian bistro for a slice of

ଓ

pizza and a soda. Other times they headed east, toward the finer stores, so Meeghan could satisfy her passion for clothes shopping. But tonight her mind was on getting home to be supportive of Josephine's mandatory haircut.

Throughout the day local radio stations had announced a storm warning for late afternoon. Now the steel-gray sky blended with the dingy city buildings, making the hour appear later than it actually was.

Meeghan braced herself against a gripping wind that plastered her light coat to the back of her legs. She and Bruce were forced to raise their voices above the wind, as the grit from the streets flew into their faces. Quickly the two sheltered their eyes as they moved back onto the cement steps under the alcove outside the studio door. The overhang provided three-sided protection from the elements while enabling them at the same time to watch for Meeghan's ride.

Bruce heard his name called. He turned and saw his best friend coming towards him from across the street. He and Meeghan watched incredulously as the young man not only battled the wind, but dangerously dodged the oncoming traffic with the grace and precision of a gazelle. He wove in and out, ignoring a cab driver's honking horn, as he hurried across the street and hopped up onto the curb, reaching his destination with arrogant flair. Bruce hunched his shoulders to brace himself for the customary slap on the back he knew was coming and that never failed to annoy him.

"Hey, bro, what's happen'n?" The young man was looking at Meeghan as he slapped his hand on his friend's back.

"Hey, Dante, what's up, man?" Bruce greeted, falling into the familiar urban lingo.

"Not much, bro. I'm on my way back from a research project for school. You headed home? I'll walk with you."

"Thanks, but I'm going to hang here for a bit," Bruce said, maneuvering himself in front of Meeghan.

His friend was dressed in a pair of black jeans with a white pullover sweater, its sleeves pulled up over his muscular forearms. Over the sweater he wore a red vest with a designer label sewn over the breast pocket. A shiny sterling silver cuff on his wrist flashed quickly as he extended his hand past Bruce's hip.

"Hi. Dante Alexander, Bruce's neighbor." A warm brown hand encircled Meeghan's cold thumb in urban welcome.

"Hello. Meggie O'Dell, Bruce's dance partner." She felt the blood rush up from her neck, hoping the tone of her voice had made it clear that Bruce was not her boyfriend.

Still clutching her thumb, Dante opened his fingers and, like a Venus flytrap, quickly enveloped Meeghan's entire hand. Her breath caught in her throat, and she laughed, her stomach plummeting, as if she were on a roller coaster ride.

The boy was standing close enough for her to detect a subtle scent of Sandalwood on his skin, which momentarily drifted like gossamer between them. Within seconds it was lost amidst the city's smells, but not before Meeghan had inhaled it. It was like an aphrodisiac. The heady sensation of sensual attraction played havoc with her equilibrium and made her quiver.

Dante smiled. "Are you cold?"

"No. Yes. A little, I guess." She was lost in his eyes, which at this moment reflected the city lights.

"So, *Meggie...*" Dante said, still holding her hand, still drawing her in. "Do you live here in Manhattan?"

"N-no," she stammered. "I live in Waterbridge, north of here."

"I know it well. You've got some phenomenal old buildings in that town." He saw she looked pleased. "Our architecture class went there last year to sketch," he told her.

"Yeah, Dante goes to Columbia," Bruce said, trying to cut in on the conversation. "He's breaking a lot of campus hearts."

"That's not entirely true," Dante denied, flashing a bashful smile. His teeth were so white and even, no one could deny they had been exposed to professional orthodontia.

"Columbia. That's impressive," Meeghan replied.

Bruce guffawed. "His parents can afford it, they're both orthodontists."

That explains the teeth, Meeghan thought.

The wind had increased and was now blowing haphazardly across the avenues. It continued to kick up debris and occasionally slap it like stickers onto unsuspecting passersby.

It blew a silky black ringlet of Dante's hair in front of his eyes. He pushed it away with his hand and tucked it behind his ear only to have the curl defiantly pop out again. Meeghan thought she had never seen anything so endearing. She wished she could reach out to touch those shiny curls and smooth them away from his forehead.

She thought his face was the most beautiful she had ever seen. His chiseled nose and high cheekbones were particularly fascinating to her. They were not typical features for a black man, but suggested a Caucasian parent. His skin, the color of which reminded her of the coffee lattes she was so fond of, was as thick and smooth as polished stone. Meeghan found herself yearning to touch his face.

The three of them stood at the corner as traffic crawled, horns honked, and pedestrians rushed to flag taxis and catch subways and trains, all in an effort to find shelter before the storm hit.

Dante hung one arm around his friend's shoulders while he rubbed his knuckles atop Bruce's head. "We're playing basketball tonight at the gym. If you're not too tired, you want to play, 'Little Bro?'" He pointed his thumb at Bruce and said to Meeghan, "He absolutely hates when I call him that. But I'm his elder by three years, so he has to put up with me."

"No, I don't!" Bruce snapped. He was sorry Dante had happened by and sorrier still that he had met Meeghan. Now he just wanted to see him go. "Maybe I'll play, okay? Why don't you call me before you leave?"

"I'll do that," Dante said.

Bruce purposely turned his back, and Dante took the hint. He smiled at Meeghan. "It was nice meeting you," he said. "Maybe I'll see you around here again some time."

"I take this class Mondays, Wednesdays, and Fridays." She hoped his memory was sharp.

"I'll watch for you when I'm passing by."

A few heavy raindrops began to fall. Like a tear, one of them splattered on Dante's cheek, causing him to blink. Perhaps he knew it only added to his charm, for he let it hang there like a diamond on his skin.

"Look, Meggie," said Bruce, anxious for her attention. "Here comes your ride!"

"So it is." Meeghan glanced at her wristwatch. She was reluctant to leave. She figured it to be just her luck that Mr. McGlynn would arrive right on schedule, on this of all days.

Bruce hurried to get her backpack from the steps and opened the car door so Meeghan could get in before it started to rain.

"Thanks!" she called out above the wind, taking the bag from him and tossing it in the car. "I'll see you on Wednesday!" Her hair whipped across her face as she turned to say goodbye to Dante, but he had already disappeared somewhere in the crowd of pedestrians.

Josephine had parked the car in the garage and was running toward the house when the skies opened up to let the rain pelt down in a heavy torrent. She bounded through the front door, nearly tripping over Beau, and quickly slipped out of her coat. Her hands reached up to touch her head, and once again she felt the deep pang of regret.

Beau cringed and growled as Josephine picked him up, the black beady eyes that peered out from beneath two shaggy brows intently focused on a face that smelled familiar but which he did not recognize.

"Come on, Beau—it's Mommy. Don't be afraid."

The thunderstorm had clearly unnerved the animal. As he was lowered to the floor, he began to jump up and down, spinning around in a circle and barking incessantly before fleeing from the room. The dog's rejection only helped to heighten Josephine's rapidly-deflating self image. Upstairs she nearly collided with Mary, who was putting away the laundry in the master bedroom.

"Why, Ma'am, you gave me a fright!" Mary exclaimed, clasping a stack of clothes to her chest. When she recovered, she said, "Aren't you just looking like a young girl with that haircut?"

"More like a young *boy*," Josephine said sheepishly.

Mary walked around her and assessed the haircut with a critical eye. "I declare, it looks as though the doctor has two daughters, he does!"

"Do you really think Liam will like it?"

"He will like it all right because it's his love that's wearing it." She patted Josephine with a pudgy hand that smelled of lemons. "Now don't worry about the doctor's likes and dislikes, you hear? If you're worrying about anything, it should be about becoming too thin," she clucked. "You'll be pleased to know, I made your favorite dessert this morning."

"Cheesecake?" Josephine tried to sound enthused, even though she was not in the least bit hungry.

"Yes, and I'll be expecting you to eat a good portion of it tonight."

In the sanctuary of her bedroom Josephine kicked off her shoes and dropped down, in a heap, on top of the coverlet.

Mary returned with another stack of folded laundry. "You will need to fold down that comforter, or else the feathers will be flattening," she lectured.

Josephine groaned, too fatigued to move. But Mary was not to be ignored. She lifted Josephine's shoulders first, then her hips, pulling the comforter down and then spreading it over her like a fluffy cloud. "Now there, isn't that just a wee bit better?"

"Yes, thank you." Josephine closed her eyes. "Did Patrick leave on time today? I don't want Meggie standing outside waiting in this weather."

"Aye, he'll be on time, or he'll be accounting to me." Mary closed the drapes against the depressing gloom of a stormy late afternoon. "I'll wake you then when dinner is ready."

CR

# CHAPTER *Fourteen*

By the way she fidgeted at the dinner table and picked at her food, it was obvious Meeghan had a boy on her mind. Her father, however, was oblivious. He was annoyed that his wife was sleeping through dinner when he had planned to discuss her first chemotherapy treatment, which was scheduled for the following morning.

Father and daughter sat at the dinner table, both lost in their own thoughts and each withholding what was on their mind in exchange for polite chitchat. Liam gave a trivial account of his day, which Meeghan all but ignored. He tried asking about her dance class only to receive answers in one-word syllables. Within a matter of minutes the two had run the conversational gamut, after which Meeghan stared dreamily into space while her father sat brooding.

When dessert was brought to the table, Liam cut large slices of cheesecake for himself and another for Meeghan, in a subconscious effort to bond through culinary decadence.

At the base of Meeghan's chair, Beau had sat through the entire meal like a black statue, his eyes transfixed on the table top. He had followed each forkful from plate to mouth in hopes a morsel might fall from someone's fork onto the carpet. From the corner of his eye he saw his competition enter the room as Mrs. McGlynn came through the swinging door to clear the table with Sundae in tow. The cat followed so closely in step beside her, it could have passed for a furry slipper on the old woman's foot.

In cautious observance of the dog, Sundae disappeared under the table to reap immediate reward by licking the oriental carpet clean of the few select dinner crumbs the dog had obviously overlooked.

Upstairs Josephine awakened from a bout of sweats. She climbed out of bed and undressed, slipping into a light nightshirt. The clock on the night stand reminded her she had slept past supper, and she toyed with the idea of going downstairs to make herself a plate of food, but her appetite was absent.

When Meeghan came up stairs, she found her stepmother sitting at the dressing table. The table lamp cast a golden glow behind Josephine's head and across her shoulders. She appeared waif-like in the over-sized nightshirt, with her hair cropped as short as a boy's.

"Oh, my God!" Meeghan exclaimed, laughing nervously. "You really did it!"

"I sure did. I know it's short, but do you like it?"

The teen cocked her head and scrutinized. She wrinkled her nose and pursed her lips. "I was used to your long hair," she admitted frankly, "but this is okay."

"This *is* my long hair," Josephine said, "compared to what I'm going to have once I start the chemo. What do you think your father will say?"

"About what?" Liam entered the room, engrossed in the latest stock report. He sat down on the side of the bed, the top of his graying head crowning above the newspaper. He heard Josephine clear her throat, and he looked up. "Oh, wow! You've cut your hair!"

Meeghan rolled her eyes at her stepmother in concurrence of the insensitivity of men.

"I thought it best, seeing as how it won't be on my head in a few weeks," Josephine said. "Do you like it?"

"It's...um, nice...very becoming." He didn't like it at all, but he knew better than to say so.

"Really?" she asked again, but Liam had already retreated to the bathroom.

An ominous crash of thunder brought both dog and cat scampering into the bedroom in search of sanctuary. Beau nearly leapt into Meeghan's outstretched arms while Sundae jumped silently on the bed to hide under the covers.

"I'm sorry I missed dinner tonight," Josephine apologized. "I heard Mary made cheesecake."

"Mmm, it was good, too," Meeghan confirmed. "I'll have to dance extra hard to work it off." She sat on the bed waiting for Josephine to finish applying night cream to her face and throat. Another clap of thunder broke, and an already frightened dog shook in her arms. The table lamp flickered.

Josephine finished her moisturizing routine and rose to join her stepdaughter on the edge of the bed. "How was dance class today?"

"Hard."

"That's good. How can you ever hope to become accomplished without working hard for it? Besides, a relentless dance instructor ensures that the Christmas recital will be a great success. It also will ensure that you will dance in the first lineup." She wondered why Meeghan was lingering when she herself longed to go back to bed.

Liam had come out of the bathroom, lifting Beau from his daughter's arms. "I'm not looking forward to taking him out in this," he grumbled, and walked out of the room holding the dog like a sack of potatoes.

When she was sure her father was out of earshot, Meeghan said, "I met a boy today. His name is Dante. He's a freshman at Columbia University."

"Really? And where did you meet him? You know Dad and I forbid you to talk to strangers in the city."

"He's not a stranger, he's Bruce Spanelli's neighbor. He walked by while we were waiting for my ride."

Josephine saw through the casual façade to the starry look in her stepdaughter's eyes. "And how old is this *boy*?"

"Eighteen, I think."

"He's too old for you, Meggie; you haven't even begun dating yet."

"I'm not dating..."

"And you're not about to start," Liam chimed in as he re-entered the room with a damp dog at his heels. "What's all this about?"

"Nothing," Meeghan sulked.

"She's met an eighteen year old," Josephine informed him, crossing her arms across her chest in disapproval.

"I just *met* him, I didn't marry him!"

"Watch that tone, miss!" her father admonished.

Meeghan jabbed her finger toward Josephine. "She's the one making a federal case out of this!"

"I merely said the boy is too old for you. He's already in college."

"I agree with Josephine. I would never consider you seeing a college student, Meeghan," Liam said sternly.

"We're just *friends*!"

"Not even as a friend. I'm adamant about this."

"Oh, my God, I don't believe the two of you! You're from the dark ages!" Meeghan cried, jumping from the bed.

"And you're out of control!" Liam thundered.

Josephine had crawled into bed unnoticed. She wasn't up to doing battle. She rolled over on her side, only too willing to let Liam handle his daughter, although she felt guilty sticking him with the issue she had initiated.

Meeghan was intent on pushing her point. "All I did was mention I met a guy, and right away I'm told I can't see him. Why am I always treated as if I'm a baby?"

"No one said you couldn't see him. We said you can't date him, whoever he is." Her father's patience was wearing thin.

"His name is Dante. He's Bruce's best friend, and his parents are both orthodontists," she added.

"I don't care if they are the President and First Lady. You're not dating David, or Donald, or anybody else for that matter!"

"So what am I supposed to do if he's with Bruce when I'm there?"

"Okay, Meeghan, enough of this!" Liam commanded. "I'm tired, and Josephine has her treatment tomorrow. We all need to get some rest. Have you done your homework tonight?"

"I hardly have any," Meeghan snapped, annoyed at being dismissed.

"Well I suggest you get to it then. And don't go to bed too late, you hear?" But Meeghan had already left the room with Beau following on her heels.

"Come back and shut our door, please!" Liam shouted, but to no avail. He was forced to get out of bed and close the door himself, trying at the same time to retrieve the cat from under the covers; however, Sundae scampered out ahead of his reach, jumped off the bed and hid beneath it. "Fine!" he grumbled. "Stay there, I don't care."

He shuffled back to the bed, stepped out of his slippers and climbed in under the covers. He wrapped his arm around Josephine and moved closer, molding the front of his lanky body against the back of hers in perfect spoon fashion. He thought she felt abnormally warm.

"I like your haircut, I really do," he whispered, kissing the back of her neck.

"No, you don't. You hate it." She threw his arm from her waist.

"You know I think you're beautiful," he crooned. "Why not scoot your hips back a little?"

But Josephine was not to be coaxed or cajoled with. The upcoming chemo treatment had her tense, and the thought of losing her hair made her feel unfeminine. If that wasn't enough to kill any chance of romance, there was Meeghan's tirade.

Liam tried again. "Are you sure I can't talk you into a little lovemaking? Technically we're still newlyweds, you know."

"I'm not feeling particularly desirable tonight, if you don't mind. Turn out the light, will you?"

"Okay, I understand if you're not feeling well."

"Do you, Liam?"

"Do I what?"

"Understand? Tell me how you can possibly understand how I'm feeling. That I'm terrified because tomorrow I'm going to be injected with chemicals that will ignite my insides like the fourth of July; that

I'm constantly having sweats and mood swings, but I can't take any hormones because I have cancer; that I feel skinny, unfeminine, and unattractive; and that if I wasn't so afraid of dying, I'd wish I were dead! Can you understand all that, Liam?"

Liam lay perfectly still, his libido depleted by the verbal onslaught. He knew from past experience that whenever Josephine carried on this way, nothing he could say would elevate her mood. More importantly, he wondered how they were going to survive what they were in for once she began her treatments.

In total stillness, their single silhouette was cast on the wall by the soft glow from the table lamp. Finally Liam turned over and turned off the light.

Sometime during the night, when she was sure the rain had subsided, Sundae snuck out from her hiding place under the bed. She arched her back in a high stretch and stalked across the room on silent paws. In two strides she jumped once onto the chair, and then again on top of Liam's dresser where she perched for her customary watch in the peace and serenity of the darkness.

ↄ

# CHAPTER *Fifteen*

On the morning of her stepdaughter's sixteenth birthday, Josephine sat in bed reading a book on cancer wellness. Kathy Knoeller, the cancer therapist assigned to Josephine by the hospital, impressed upon her patient the importance of a positive attitude, of convincing one's body that the chemotherapy was destroying all existing cancer cells.

Kathy's maternal personality evoked confidence in all of her patients. She was knowledgeable, compassionate and had a remarkable sense of humor. Lately she had been the only person capable of putting a smile on Josephine's face and a flicker of hope in her heart. It was because of her counseling that Josephine was able to put aside her health issues to help with the plans for Meeghan's surprise party.

Amelia and her mother had offered to house the party, and Josephine was in charge of sending the invitations. Apart from a list of classmates from school, party guests included a few friends from Meeghan's dance class and Dante Alexander. Josephine didn't remember which had been more difficult: convincing Liam to allow Dante to be invited, or persuading Bruce to give her his friend's phone number.

She had seen to it that the second of her chemo treatments was administered two weeks prior to the party to ensure her feeling well enough to participate. True to what Dr. Chan had told her, Josephine reacted to the chemicals exactly as was predicted. The administering nurse would give her a sedative to help her sleep while the chemical cocktail dripped through the Port-A-Cath. This time she hadn't been able to sleep through the treatment and had actually felt her insides growing hot as the chemicals coursed through her veins.

By the time she had left the hospital, she felt as though her body was sending off electric shocks—tingling sensations that invaded certain parts of her body. Like a conductor of electricity, Josephine felt as if she literally *glowed.*

Within thirty-six hours, the nausea and vomiting had begun, followed days later by her hair falling out in clumps. She lost all of it, including her eyelashes and eyebrows within the first five weeks.

Normally, it would have been all too degrading, except for Kathy Knoeller teaching Josephine to laugh at herself as often as she was able. "Humor," Kathy told her, "deflects the negative and increases the positive." Her doctrine of *gratitude, not attitude* encouraged Josephine to continue the fight to live without harboring self-pity or resentment.

More than her desire to have a long life with Liam, Josephine wanted to watch Meeghan grow up. She felt the child especially needed her during these important teenage years. Her prayer each day was that God would keep her on earth long enough to see Meeghan through college, though secretly she wished for far greater time than that. For the time being, she was grateful simply to be a part of her stepdaughter's sixteenth birthday celebration.

The plan was that Liam and David would leave early on the day of the party to drive their daughters to Connecticut for an equestrian event. It wasn't Meeghan's idea of how to spend her birthday, but Amelia had just begun riding again, and Meeghan knew her being there was important to her.

The birthday cake was to be made from scratch, and when Josephine entered the kitchen, Mary had already spread out all the ingredients and utensils needed.

"Good morning," the cook greeted. "Are you ready to do some baking with me?"

"I'm all yours," Josephine saluted, placing the neck band of a large white apron over her head and fumbling with the apron's ties.

Mary gently pushed her hands away. "Let me do that for you." Deftly she tied a big bow behind Josephine's small waist, grimacing at the woman's emaciation.

"All right then," Josephine said, ready to work, "our Meggie wants pineapple cake? Pineapple cake, it will be!"

In keeping with the party theme *Surfing in Hawaii*, they baked the cake and iced it in a butter cream icing. Then they decorated it with authentic tropical orchids, which had been shipped overnight by the Silvermans.

Meanwhile, next door, Laura orchestrated the small crew who came to set up the tiki bar with its thatched roof. It came equipped with a service bar on which Laura stationed two blenders for virgin cocktails. There was a cooler filled with soft drinks, juices and bottled water, and the deck had been cleared for dancing. Around the railing they had strung colorful tiki lights where the hired DJ would be playing music.

Rental chairs and a few tables had been placed outside. These were for the bowls of corn chips, salsa, and mixed nuts that would later be brought out. She had carved a watermelon and filled it with fresh fruit and prepared a platter of shrimp plus another of assorted cheeses. The picnic table stood ready in preparation for the six-foot hero sandwich and baked ziti to be served once the party was underway.

Josephine had promised Liam she would take a nap in the afternoon, but sleep did not come easily for her. In the distance she could hear the boisterous bellowing of the Barnard twins as they arrived home after spending the better part of the day at a neighbor's. Reluctantly she closed her eyes and tried to concentrate on her wellness exercises. Eventually she managed to doze off, despite her annoyance at having forgotten to buy herself a Hawaiian-print head scarf to wear to the party.

It was an evening made to order. A wind from the northwest arrived in time to push away the humidity so that the weather remained cool and comfortable. Thirty teenage guests, each wearing colorful plastic leis around their necks, caroused in the pool or danced on the deck and on the lawn. The students from Meeghan's dance class were easy to identify by their ability to move with undeniable talent to the beat of the music.

Amelia looked incredibly happy as she danced, her blond hair whipping about her head, and her shapely arms flailing in the air as she partnered with Bruce for a rap song. Not only had she become self-confident since her surgery, but her young body had matured.

Meeghan was beside her, dancing with a boy from her high school. She looked every bit the birthday girl in a strapless, blue Hawaiian print mini-dress, with sandals, and a choker necklace and ankle bracelet made of tiny white seashells.

Her long brown hair, which had grown well below her shoulders, caught the highlights of the tiki lights and glistened in a shiny mass beneath a crown of pink orchids.

The transformation from the withdrawn, hefty adolescent of a year ago to the lovely young woman gyrating on the lawn, was amazing to behold.

Liam and Josephine sat off to the side at a table with Laura and David, conversing between periodic interruptions from the twins. There were idle threats of early bedtime if the boys didn't behave, until eventually the brothers tired of being ignored and went inside to watch TV.

By eleven o'clock, Josephine had reached her limit, but she was determined to hold up until the cake was served at midnight. She rested her head on the back of her lounge chair, struggling to stay awake. Laura noticed and saw to it that the dessert was brought out earlier so that Josephine could watch Meeghan blow out her candles. The cake was a hit with the teens, many of them hinting for a second helping. But to Josephine's chemically-sensitive taste buds, her slice tasted metallic and flavorless.

When Liam caught her yawning, he insisted on escorting his wife home to go to bed. Josephine argued to stay to watch the opening of gifts and to help Laura with some of the cleanup, but Liam all but lifted her bodily out of the chair. He held her arm as they made their way through the maze of teenagers until they found their daughter with Dante among a small group of friends.

"Meggie, say goodnight to Josephine; I'm taking her home."

Meeghan turned to her parents. Her face was flushed and radiant with exertion and the excitement of the evening. "Josie, this was *the best* birthday ever! Thank you for my cake and presents, whatever you got me." She wrapped her arms around her stepmother and pulled her close. Josephine winced with pain.

"I'm so sorry. Did I hurt you?"

"Not at all," Josephine lied. "I'm glad you're having such a good time. It was awfully good of Amelia and her mother to do this for you."

"I know. They're the greatest!"

Josephine gave Dante a warm smile and extended her hand. "It was nice to finally meet you."

"Likewise," Dante replied, gently taking Josephine's hand and holding it for several seconds.

Before kissing her stepmother goodnight, Meeghan moved closer to whisper in her ear. "Isn't he everything I said he was?" She turned to her father. "Good night, Daddy."

"I'm not going to bed," Liam corrected. "I'm coming back to keep an eye on you, so you had better behave." His looked directly at Dante, but the young man was not intimidated.

"Thanks for inviting me, Mrs. O'Dell. It was nice meeting you both."

"You're welcome, Dante. We hope you enjoyed yourself. Perhaps we'll see you again sometime?"

"Yes, thank you. I hope you feel better very soon."

Dante stood firm, his muscular arms folded comfortably across his chest as he watched Meeghan's parents walk away. "I don't think your father likes me."

"My stepmom does. She'll turn Dad around."

"What is it? Is it about my being mixed?"

"Don't be ridiculous," Meeghan bristled. "It's not about that. It was the age thing. I wasn't allowed to date until I turned sixteen."

"So, now you can?"

"I think so, if someone was to ask me, that is," she said, coquettishly. Her green eyes were hiding demurely beneath their dark lashes.

"Sixteen year old girls don't need daddy's permission?"

"Before tonight I would have thought you needed Bruce's permission." Meeghan glanced across the lawn where Bruce stood with his arm around Amelia. "But now it looks like he's interested in Amelia, not me."

"Bruce likes her a lot," Dante affirmed. He leaned in to whisper in her ear, bringing with him the familiar scent of sandalwood. "You see? He's acting like an idiot, which translated, means he's in love."

"No, seriously, how do you know?" Meeghan asked.

"He told me earlier. He thinks she's beautiful and very brave to have gone through what she did."

"Yes, she is brave...and wonderful. I'm not surprised Bruce has feelings for her."

"You sound disappointed."

"I'm not. Bruce is awesome and the best dance partner ever, but I could never be in love with him."

"That's good, because someone else has designs on you."

"Oh? And who would that be?"

"Don't act like you didn't know," Dante said, tapping the tip of her nose with his finger.

"Let's just say I've been hoping." Meeghan glanced down to admire the sterling silver cuff that shone on her wrist. It had been Dante's birthday gift to her.

"Do you like the bracelet?" he asked.

"I love it! It's very special. Thank you."

"Bruce told me once that you admired mine."

"Hey, don't change the subject," Meeghan said. "Were you about to ask me out just a minute ago?"

"Maybe. And if I did, would you agree to go out with me?"

"I would."

"Great. My parents are taking the family to Bermuda next week. I can call you as soon as I get back."

"Oh." Meeghan's disappointment was apparent.

"Not to worry. I'll be back in ten days, and then we'll make a date. Okay?"

"Sure, if you don't meet someone else in Bermuda."

"Not me. I'm already spoken for."

"Really? Who's the lucky girl?"

"Oh, just some girl I know who just happens to wear a silver cuff like mine."

The DJ was calling the last song, and many of the guests had paired off together. Amelia looked over at Meeghan and grinned before placing her hands on Bruce's shoulders and giving herself up to the romance of a slow dance.

Dante took Meeghan in his arms. "Can I have this last dance?" They were lost in the moment until Dante spotted Liam's tall figure walking toward them. "Dear old Dad is headed this way," he warned. "How much you want to bet he cuts in on us?"

"He wouldn't dare," Meeghan said, wrapping her arms around his neck. The sterling cuff shone brightly on her wrist. "I'm the birthday girl, remember? I get to make the choices tonight!"

Lights of every color danced like fairies upon her creamy shoulders while the hollow in her throat housed a shadow Dante longed to kiss, and would have, had her father not been so near.

For the first time Meeghan felt the power of herself as a female, aware of the spell she was weaving. She pressed her body against Dante's until they were melded together from chest to knees, caring not at all about the disapproving scowl on her father's face, or what he'd have to say to her when the party was over.

It was evident that the events of the night before had taken their toll on Josephine. Liam insisted she spend Sunday resting while he went to church and then to the hospital to make his rounds.

Alone in her chair in the family room, she was lonely with Liam gone and Meeghan still in bed. Even Mary was out, having left to run errands with her husband. Had it not been for a phone call from Laura, or for Beau lying devotedly at her feet, she might have felt abandoned.

Her breakfast tray lay set aside, untouched except for a bite of toast and a few sips of coffee she had taken with which to wash down two Tylenol. Mary would have something to say about the uneaten meal when she came home. It frustrated the housekeeper to see Josephine failing to regain the weight she had lost and was still continuing to lose.

The armchair, with its high back and overstuffed arms, appeared to envelop Josephine's slender form as she worked on her laptop in an attempt to answer e-mails from friends and well-wishers. She knew that the numbness in her fingertips was a direct reaction to the chemo, but Dr. Chin had told her the feeling would return once the treatments were finished. For now the lack of sensation made it difficult for her to use the keyboard with any level of efficiency.

Meeghan came down the stairs with the grace of a bull elephant. She appeared at the bottom landing looking like a sleepwalker, her eyes half closed and her hair in total disarray. She spotted Josephine and emitted some form of inaudible greeting before disappearing into the dining room. She came back out a few minutes later with a plate of fresh fruit and a mug of hot tea. Her feet were shoved into fuzzy purple slippers, which grated across the floors as if the soles were made of sandpaper.

Josephine stopped what she was doing and shut down her computer. "Good morning, Cinderella."

"Morning. How are you feeling?" Meeghan asked.

"Not much change with me these days. I'm plugging along. How about you? Have you recuperated from last night?"

"Sort of."

"Did you have a good time? What kind of presents did you get? I'd love to see them."

"I'll show you later."

"So, were you surprised?"

"Like, my heart stopped beating when I walked in their back yard," Meeghan said, picking a fresh strawberry from her plate and biting into it.

"Pretty cool of me to get Dante there, didn't you think?" Josephine was proud of herself for coercing Liam into agreeing to invite the young man.

"Totally. Amelia told me you did that. Thanks."

"What did Dante give you?"

Meeghan held up her wrist, pulling back her pajama sleeve to display the new silver wrist cuff. "It's engraved with my initials and birth date."

"That's quite a gift!" Josephine inspected the bracelet more closely. "Initials, too, eh? Nice. It looks like the kind of gift that says Dante plans to see you again."

"So he says..."

"You don't sound very excited."

"I am," Meeghan sighed. "It's just that he's going away on vacation with his family, and I won't be able to see him until he gets back."

"Which will be when?"

"In about ten days," she said wistfully. "Dad doesn't like him, does he?"

"He doesn't dislike him."

"First he didn't want me dating until I was sixteen. Now what's his problem? Dante thinks it's because he's part black."

"You know better than to think your father would ever be prejudiced, Meggie."

"So then, why was he so rude every time Dante tried to talk to him last night? It made him very uncomfortable, the way Dad acted like he was angry, or something."

"If he looked angry, which he wasn't," Josephine said, "it's because he's worried."

"About?"

"He's worried about your infatuation with Dante—with any boy for that matter. He wants you to concentrate on your future. You're going to be graduating next year."

"I'm concentrating. I already know what I want to major in."

"That's good. And the trip to Ireland with your dance class this summer will look very good on your transcript. But you need to begin focusing, zeroing in on where you'd like to go."

"I've thought it might be kind of cool to study in Ireland, like Dad did, but I'm not sure." She blew into the cup of hot tea, and the herbal scent surrounded them.

"M-m-m, your tea smells good," Josephine said. She lifted a hand to her forehead to feel whether or not the fever had gone down.

"Would you like a cup? I'll go get it for you."

"Maybe in a little while, not right now."

Meeghan sat on the ottoman beside her stepmother. She ran a cool hand affectionately over Josephine's stubby scalp and then held her hand. "You don't look good at all, and your head feels like a porcupine's."

"Thanks a lot."

"Sorry. I'm worried about you."

"Don't worry; I'm fine."

"And what if you're not?"

"The doctors are right on top of this thing. I'm going to finish these awful chemo treatments, and then I'll have the surgery to check to make sure they got all the cancer cells."

Meeghan frowned. "What do you mean? How do they check that? What do they do?"

"They go in surgically and take biopsies to make sure all the cancer cells are gone. I'll have a catheter inserted in my abdomen so that they can flush out my insides and watch for any positive cells...those are the bad ones."

"Oh, yuck!" Meeghan nervously kneaded Josephine's hand, but her stepmother stilled her.

"Meggie..."

"No, please, no more." Meeghan lowered her head and began to cry.

"Meggie, Meggie," Josephine soothed. "Listen, you mustn't be afraid."

"But I am!"

"What is it you fear, sweetheart?"

Meeghan's answer was a stifled sob.

"Are you afraid I am going to die?"

"Yes."

"Some days I'm afraid of that, too. But I have to believe that God is going to put me where He wants me to be."

"But I want Him to want you to be with me! You just got here!"

"I want to be with you and your father, too, Meggie, but unfortunately, we don't get to make that decision, do we?"

"I don't know what I'd do if anything happened to you."

"You'd find your way. You're much stronger than you give yourself credit for."

"If that's true, it's because you're here with me."

"No, Meggie. Perhaps I helped, but it was you who lost the weight and became a dancer. It was you who has built your character. You're the captain of your own ship, and the ship you are sailing is your own destiny. It has nothing to do with me."

Meeghan sat up and dried her eyes on her pajama sleeve. She pulled two tissues from the box on the table and loudly blew her nose. "If I'm the captain, then you're my navigator," she said, pleased with her own analogy.

"A captain can sail her ship without a navigator," Josephine countered. "She just follows the stars and trusts that God will bring her home safely." She wanted to change the subject. "So, what do you say? How about you show me what your friends gave you for your birthday?"

"I want to shower first."

"Okay."

Meeghan stood up with her plate in hand. She was walking out of the room when she turned and looked at the woman she had come to know and love. "Maybe you're right," she said. "Maybe a captain can sail her ship home by way of the stars. But what you don't understand is that there can be no home for the captain if she has no mother waiting there to hear about her adventures at sea!"

# CHAPTER *Sixteen*

Josephine's chemotherapy treatments ended before Thanksgiving and were followed with a successful second surgery. Ira Goldstein sent her home from the hospital with a paper prescription instructing her to enjoy the holidays. He advised that after the New Year, she should be seen at regular intervals for the usual CA-125 blood tests. However, with Liam and Kyoto Chin, Ira spoke on a professional level. They knew, as medical doctors, that there was no cure for cancer once the major organs were involved. The best they could offer was to hope the treatments had bought Josephine a fair amount of remission and to have an alternative plan of action when the insidious disease recurred.

A clean bill of health gave their patient a new lease on life. With the holidays upon them and Josephine's health stabilized, the O'Dells accepted as many social invitations as they could. In November, Meeghan's Christmas dance recital was held in an off-Broadway theatre. It was the highlight of the season. The dance troupe was remarkable, and the audience of parents and friends sat rooted to their seats, mesmerized by the synchronization of those young men and women who had, up until that night, been thought of only as children.

To the throngs of a standing ovation, Meeghan took her bows with the poise and grace of a professional. Josephine thought her heart would burst with love and pride while Liam applauded until his hands were sore. Dante and Amelia stood to cheer, their victory cries drowned out by the rowdy and boisterous rallying of the Bernard clan.

Denis O'Shea came out last to take his bows and announce to the audience his plan to take his young troupe to Ireland for two weeks during the summer. Cost would be partially defrayed through fund raising; the purpose of the trip being to familiarize the students with their heritage, as well as to study the foundation of the dance he hoped by now had become a part of their very souls. Again the audience gave a thunderous ovation, and Denis O'Shea felt sure that every parent present would be willing and eager to help fund the trip abroad for their son or daughter.

The recital was the talk about town for days afterward. Perhaps it was the thrill of it, or the witnessing of Meeghan's transformation from chubby teen to feminine young woman. Whatever the reason, Josephine knew that more than anything in the world, she wanted to survive her illness in order to be a part of Meeghan's life. With her chemotherapy treatments finished, she wanted Liam's opinion regarding her life expectancy if and when the CA-125 came back positive. She knew she could count on him to be honest with her.

"How long?" Josephine asked one evening, taking her husband by surprise.

Had it been any other patient, Liam could have answered with detached emotion. But it was his wife asking, and his heart was involved.

"From the time we get a positive report? I'm not sure. It's difficult to calculate these things."

"Please try."

"I don't know, but I would guess not long."

"How long, Liam?"

"Without treatment? A few weeks...a month, perhaps."

The silence between them rocked their world. Liam knew the moment was now for him to offer words of encouragement. Instead, it was Josephine who came forward to wrap her arms around her husband's broad shoulders and held him while he broke down and cried.

If she allowed herself to fantasize, Josephine could almost fool herself into believing she was going to live. Her appetite had returned with what she termed a *vengeance*. Food was no longer tasteless to her, and she once again could fully appreciate Mary's culinary abilities. Her hair, too, had grown in, although a different color and texture. She scheduled another appointment with Yvonne to have it styled for the holidays and relished informing her that she'd be making appointments on a regular basis.

The plan was to spend New Year's Eve with their group at The Clapton Inn. Meeghan, who would stay at home with the McGlynns, was given permission to doubledate with Dante, Amelia, and Bruce, provided she come home shortly after midnight.

As their car sped along the Massachusetts Turnpike, Josephine felt better than she had in a long time. Her relationship with her husband had been much improved of late. She felt attractive enough to welcome Liam's sexual advances and surprised herself by occasionally being the one to initiate the lovemaking between them.

Weight loss was still an issue for her, although it had leveled off, and her taste buds were back to normal again. This was evident as she reached behind her for the bag of snacks she had packed. She fumbled for two polished Granny Smith apples, handing one to Liam as they traveled the seemingly endless miles of interstate and sang along to the oldies on the radio.

When they reached the Clapton village, Liam drove to the *Pocketful of Posies* so Josephine could see how the window had been decorated for Christmas. Nostalgia welled up inside her for the town she had called home for so many years. She and Liam got out of the car and stepped up on the curb to view the winter wonderland behind the glass.

There were evergreens sprayed with artificial snow and holly bushes with tiny winter birds nestled in their berried branches. A three-foot angel dressed in ivory robes had been suspended from the ceiling by invisible thread. Her arms were open wide, seemingly to be shedding grace upon the miniature woodland animals strategically positioned in secluded spots along the floor of an imaginary thicket.

In a small clearing of make-believe snow was a manger housing ceramic statues of the holy family: Joseph, Mary, and the baby Jesus lying in the wooden cradle. Paying homage beside him was a statue of Santa kneeling on one knee. He was holding his red cap to his breast; his balding head was bent in humble reverence for the Christ child, wrapped in swaddling clothes, whose infant arms were raised and opened in a universal blessing.

It was the materialistic icon of Christmas, bowing before the spiritual one, with a message so profound as to render both Liam and Josephine speechless. They stood hand in hand on the empty sidewalk, their breath releasing warm vapors into the frigid air.

Liam noticed his wife's solemn expression and wondered if she was missing her old job. How could he know that she was, at this very moment, filled with a divine grace that delivered her from her fear of dying? How could he know that when he took her arm and they walked away from the scene, Josephine would be completely filled with peace?

☙

"This lamb is outrageous!" Marsha exclaimed, daintily holding a tiny loin lamb chop between two fingers and nibbling the meat from the bone. "Just what is it about dining out that makes it thoroughly enjoyable?" Beneath the restaurant's low lighting, the diamond jewelry she wore flashed like camera lights as she wiped her hands on a linen napkin.

"It must be that we don't have to cook it ourselves," Alex wagered to guess. She sipped a savory Pinot Grigio before cutting into a delectable grilled swordfish steak. Tonight she looked stunning in a champagne silk dress, the color of which complemented the healthy skin tone she maintained from living near the sea.

"Personally," Josephine chimed in, "I believe it's knowing our men are paying the bill makes this stuffed quail I'm eating taste extraordinary!" Glasses were raised in salutary agreement, and Josephine joined in the toast. She looked perfect in a red wool jacket and black slacks, her cropped hair accentuating her delicate features.

Samples of entrées were passed around the table; the ladies' wine glasses were refilled while the men sipped their Glenfiddich scotches. Josephine sat with her hands under her chin, fingers intertwined, quietly observing her cherished family and friends, who entertained and laughed with one another long after their plates had been cleared away. Alex, the only one who had thought to bring her camera, asked the waiter to snap a group photograph. All eight of them huddled close, head to head, displaying toothy grins and making comic innuendo until the waiter feared he would lose his job if they did not hurry up and pose.

After dinner, drinks were served in a separate room where guests could watch the evening's televised dropping of the ball from Times Square. Josephine, ignoring the onset of stomach cramps, began explaining the project she had begun for Meeghan and asked if Alex and Marsha would help her put it together.

It was prior to countdown when the wait staff served champagne in crystal flutes. While couples moved to take seats near the television, Josephine excused herself and went to the ladies room. Behind the stall door, she sat doubled over in pain. Beads of perspiration gathered on her forehead and across the bridge of her nose. She looked at her wrist watch. It was eleven fifty-one. In a few minutes Liam would be asking someone to check on her, and Josephine didn't want anyone to discover she was ill.

The intensity of her cramps grew, causing her to lean with her head against the cool wall of the stall. Suddenly, without warning, a bout of diarrhea passed through her like a runaway train, leaving her gasping and feeling faint. She groaned, placing her forearm across the toilet paper dispenser to rest her head. She was slick with sweat and near fainting, but she managed to stay calm, taking deep breaths until the dizziness left her.

When it was over, and she was sure her legs would support her, Josephine stood to pull up her pantyhose. It was then that she noticed the blood.

"Where've you been? We thought you fell in." Ned was holding up a glass of champagne and calling to her from across the room. She felt the bile rise in her throat as she searched for an available seat.

The TV announcer was counting down, with everyone in the room joining in: "Ten, nine, eight..."

Liam had noticed his wife enter the room visibly shaken. His trained eye spotted her pallor, and in two strides, he was beside her chair. Putting his arm around her, he bent until their faces were but inches apart. He could hear her breathing was labored. "Are you all right? What's wrong?"

"Liam," Josephine whispered, gripping a fistful of his jacket sleeve. "I'm very sick. Please, take me home!"

2002

CR

# CHAPTER *Seventeen*

The corridor hummed with the changing of shifts, doctors giving orders, and visitors coming to spend time with loved ones. In contrast to the customary singing and exchanges of toasts, Josephine had rung in the New Year with an ambulance ride to Waterbridge Hospital. As she lay in the bed of her private room with haunting recollection of the night before, she awaited a visit from Ira Goldstein. The prospect of what the blood tests and CAT scan might reveal caused her slender body to shake with nervousness beneath the nearly weightless cotton covers.

She listened for the familiar sound of her husband's footsteps in the hall as she picked at a corner of the surgical tape that held her IV in place. Liam had told her he'd be with her as soon as all the test results were in, but Josephine feared he had been detained on his patient rounds.

Eventually Ira Goldstein entered her room, gently closing the door behind him and coming to stand beside her bed.

"Hello, Josie. Liam's not here yet? I paged him a while ago. I can finish my rounds and come back later, if you'd like to wait for him."

"He should have been here by now," she said, "but it looks like it's just going to be you and me. How did I do?"

"I'm afraid I don't have very good news."

"What do you mean?"

"Your CA-125 is up. It's ninety-six. The CAT shows a mass on your liver and two spots on the colon." Ira Goldstein tried offering hope where he did not feel there was any. "I've showed your pictures to Doctor Chin. He's coming tomorrow to talk to you. He's recommending surgery to remove the mass, and a colostomy, followed by chemotherapy and a series of radiation treatments." He reached out to take her hand. "I know this is devastating news. I would have preferred to have told you when Liam was here." He paused, waiting to see if she had any questions. When she didn't reply, he placed his hand on her shoulder. "Well then, I'll leave you to think about the recommendation."

She needed to find Liam. Carefully moving herself to a sitting position on the bed, Josephine slid off the mattress to stand with bare feet on the cold linoleum floor. She reached up and unhooked the IV bag from its pole and slipped it through the arm hole of her flannel bathrobe before putting it on. Carefully she re-hooked the bag back onto the pole and belted the bathrobe closed over her hospital gown. Then, slipping her feet into a pair of slippers, she held onto the pole and shuffled out of her room down the hall.

One of the nurses at the front desk asked if she needed help, but Josephine ignored her. She was on a mission, intent on finding her husband and telling him about the test results. She prayed somehow Liam could wake her from this nightmare.

She continued down the corridor until she got to the elevators. She paced back and forth, her heart skipping a beat each time the doors opened. She looked up at the clock on the wall, feeling as though time was standing still. *Where the hell is he*?

The elevator doors opened to let two women off. They smiled at her. One of them held a floral arrangement Josephine thought shoddy and unattractive, and it amazed her to think she could assess anything at a time like this.

Minutes passed without the elevator stopping at her floor. Raising a hand to her forehead, Josephine felt for the fever she was sure was spiking. Her eyes stung with tears that threatened to spill over. Frightened, bewildered and distraught, she began the shuffle back down the hall to her room.

She hadn't gotten far when she heard the elevator doors open, but this time she did not bother to turn around. The sound of the voices behind her turned her blood to ice. It was Liam, with his voice deep and serious and a female's gentle lilt that hit Josephine with what felt like a physical force.

She caught her slipper under the wheel of the IV stand in her haste to spin around. Time stood still in the seconds that she and the metal pole performed a macabre dance before she regained her balance.

Her heart was pounding; a fine sheen of perspiration set her face aglow as she stood facing her husband and Michelle Clarkson, who was dressed in a crisp white uniform that molded to her voluptuous figure like a second skin. The tension in the hall was electrifying and palpable, as the two women recognized one another.

Liam, hoping to avoid a scene, rushed to stand beside his wife. "What are you doing here?" he asked. "You shouldn't be out of bed. You remember Michelle Clarkson, I'm sure."

Michelle smiled nervously. "Hello, Josephine, how are you feeling?"

Josephine ignored her and turned to glare at her husband.

"I was looking for you. I thought you wanted to be with me when Ira read me my test results."

"I do. And here I am.

"Well, you're a little late, Doctor O'Dell."

"Why? What did Ira say?"

"In a nutshell? He told me I'm going to die."

Liam tried taking hold of his wife's arm, but she shook off his hand as if it were something abhorrent.

Michelle had been tapping the elevator button in a rush to escape. When it failed to come up right away, her eyes darted toward the stairwell. She reminded Josephine of a mouse caught in a trap. The elevator finally landed at their floor. The doors opened slowly, and Michelle rushed to slip through, disappearing like a thief in the night.

This time Liam reached for Josephine's hand. "Let me take you back to your room. I want to hear what Ira had to say."

She pulled away. "You can read his report!"

"Yes, I will. But for now I want to know what he suggested, and I also would like to know what you think."

"I told you. I think I'm dying—not that you care."

"You're being unreasonable."

"I'm being unreasonable? You step off an elevator, talking to someone I thought was out of your life, and you call me unreasonable?"

They had reached her room. Liam tried to assist her back to bed, but Josephine refused his help. He wanted to tell her she was overreacting, but he knew that would only worsen her mood. Instead he said, "I'll read Ira's reports, and we'll go from there. Don't worry, we will fight this thing together."

"Fight what thing? Are you referring to my illness, or to your infatuation with Michelle Clarkson?"

"I can help you, Josephine, but you need to be reasonable, and you need to be sensible."

Josephine looked up at him from where she lay. Her eyes were expressionless, her lips pale and dry. "I swear I haven't got the strength."

"That's not true," Liam challenged. "You're a fighter."

"No, Liam, I'm not," she said wearily. "Not anymore."

ᏇᏒ

# CHAPTER *Eighteen*

Josephine was home from the hospital only a few days when Marsha and Alex asked if they could come for the weekend to help her finish the project for Meeghan. They arrived two days later with suitcases and bags of arts and crafts supplies. As Marsha had jokingly put it, they had come to help Josephine *futz*.

Beau performed his customary welcome exhibition, barking, jumping and nipping at their feet until the guests were forced to put down their packages in order to ruffle his black coat and woo him with sweet talk.

Sundae silently slinked down the staircase where she could observe the goings on without being noticed. For a few minutes she remained virtually unseen until Marsha spotted the fat feline spying between the wooden spindles.

"Why look, it's Sundae! Hello, pussycat! Remember me?" Sundae's stance instantly changed from languid to alert. She jumped up, took one fleeting glance at the approaching woman, and scampered up the stairs, the tiny bell on her collar jingling a hasty retreat.

"That cat never has liked me," Marsha announced, turning instead to hug Josephine, who had just been released from her sister's solid embrace.

"You two must be freezing," Josephine said, putting an arm around Marsha and planting a kiss on her smooth, rosy cheek. "Patrick has the fire going, and Mary has lunch waiting."

It broke their hearts to see Josephine so wizened; in just a few weeks her decline was painfully noticeable.

"What are we having?" Alex inquired. "It was a hell of a drive, and I'm starved!"

"There's an outrageous split pea soup waiting on the stove, and ham sandwiches on homemade bread," her sister tempted. "And when you've finished that, Mary made a warm apple crisp with vanilla ice cream for dessert." She held their hands and walked with them to the dining room, thankful for the diversion their company provided and the peace she derived from their loving support.

Knowing this would be the last good time the three of them would have together, Josephine planned to make the most of it by being affectionate and inseparable during the visit. Marsha held a chair for her, and Josephine took her seat, rubbing her hands together in anticipation of the meal. Suddenly she, too, was starved—both for food and for friendship.

Dr. Liam O'Dell spent his own lunch hour behind the mahogany desk in his office. Seated across from him was Kathy Knoeller, the wellness therapist. In the months Kathy had been treating his wife, Liam had come to respect the tall unassuming woman not only as a professional, but as an equal in the field of patient concern and welfare. Now, as he sat beside her, gone was the staunch image he portrayed on the job. Humbled by his wife's recurrence of cancer, Liam was haggard; his shoulders slumped beneath the starched white medical coat.

He held his hands in despair as he spoke of Josephine's firm decision to forgo any further chemotherapy treatments and described the recommended course of pain management suggested by Doctor Chin to ensure her comfort for whatever time she had left. Kathy was an advocate of the Hospice program and suggested contacting them. She was giving Liam the information he would need when they were interrupted by a nurse knocking on the door to announce Liam's first appointment for the afternoon.

Together Liam and Kathy walked out of the office and into the hall where they shook hands and said goodbye. Reflected in their eyes was the mutual understanding that the next time they saw one another would more than likely be at the funeral of Josephine O'Dell.

The time spent with Alex and Marsha was a double-edged sword for Josephine. Emotionally it invigorated her to where she could almost forget that she was going to die. Physically, however, their visit only served to accelerate the process.

The surprise for Meeghan had been exhausting, but they completed it in three days. This was due in part to the extra helping hands of Mary McGlynn and Laura Barnard. While Meeghan was at school, the women were busy working on the kitchen island: writing, cutting, pasting, and sewing. What resulted was a large fabric-covered cardboard box that contained a memorabilia of all-time treasures. It was the ultimate gift Josephine would soon give to Meeghan when the time was right.

The departure of Marsha and Alex left the household depressingly quiet. The chill of the long winter ahead only added to the gloom of those living inside. Before leaving for work in the morning, Liam would walk Beau outdoors and Patrick kept up with the plowing of the driveway and the shoveling of the snow along the front walk. They appeared little affected by the solitude around the house, not finding their days any different during this listless winter season.

On the afternoon the company had departed, Josephine sat in her chair watching out the window as her husband walked up the drive with Beau on a leash. Liam's heated breath billowed from his nostrils and vaporized in his face, a comic comparison to the tiny puffs of exertion which escaped Beau's tiny snout as he trotted alongside his master. The sky was blue and cloudless where the sun was reflected in blinding rays against the stark white of the snow-covered ground, producing a breathtaking canvas on which nature painted a man playing with his dog.

Josephine observed Beau leaping alongside Liam, nipping at his jeans in an effort to delay their going back inside the house. The dog tangled himself between Liam's two feet, causing him to trip and nearly fall. Clever enough to know he had appealed to his master's sense of sport, Beau shot off to one side and bolted for the side lawn with Liam in hot pursuit.

They circled one another, kicking up snow, slipping and sliding until Liam finally did fall, and the dog hopped up onto his chest in a display of total victory. Liam quickly rebounded, trapping the furry ball in his gloved hands and shaking him high in the air. Clumps of snow flew from Beau's paws and underbelly as the Scottie wiggled to be freed.

Liam got up and brushed the crusty snow from his clothing. He disappeared down the driveway with Beau trotting close to his heels in hopes of a replay. Minutes later, Josephine watched them return. Liam was sorting through a stack of mail, with Beau prancing proudly behind, ever ready for another romp.

Josephine heard her husband stamp his feet on the stone landing outside the kitchen door. She listened for Mary's stern reprimand; and when it did not come, she knew Liam had remembered to wipe the dog's paws on the towel that was always left hanging on a hook in the laundry room.

Liam came to join his wife. His cheeks were apple red, and he carried a large mug of cocoa topped with whipped cream, which Mary had waiting for him. Carefully he took a seat on the couch, facing the fireplace. He lifted his stocking feet and placed them on the coffee table, crossed at the ankles. Beau entered like a trophy winner, proudly carrying his own treat from the kitchen. With a dog biscuit protruding from his jaws, he collapsed crescent-shape beside the hearth and began to devour his snack. Seconds later he slept undisturbed by the warmth of a lazy fire.

Josephine thought her husband's face, ruddy with exertion, looked exceptionally attractive as he sipped his cocoa. There was a thin moustache of whipped cream above his upper lip that she longed to wipe away with a kiss. She watched him rummage through the mail to sort it, placing bills in a pile beside him and third class material on the floor.

"Meggie's not up yet?"

"She is," Josephine replied. "She's upstairs looking for a clothing catalog. She wants to show us something."

"Something in a catalog? That sounds like trouble." Liam had traded his empty cocoa mug for a pillow behind his neck.

"The one she's looking for has a picture of the prom dress she wants," Josephine said.

"Prom dress? Aren't proms held in the spring?"

"Yes, but Meggie says many of her friends are buying their gowns now. She wants to order this dress before it sells out. She's part of the planning committee, so she thinks she has to look extra special. You know how it is with girls."

"I suppose she's going with Donald."

"Dante."

"Right."

Meeghan's bare feet could be heard running down the stairs. She was in the room with them in a matter of seconds, looking like a snow bunny in white knit stretch pants and a white turtleneck sweater. Her ponytail swung from shoulder to shoulder as she approached her parents.

"Here it is," she said breathlessly, handing the opened catalog to Josephine. She pointed to a model wearing a baby-blue taffeta dress. "Isn't it just the most beautiful dress you've ever seen?" she squealed.

"How much is it?" her father asked.

"Oh, Daddy," Meeghan said, "you haven't even looked at it, and already all you're worried about is the price!"

"No, I'm also worried about who you're planning to go with."

"Oh, here we go again...," Meeghan rolled her eyes and looked to her stepmother for support.

"Liam, at least look at the dress," Josephine suggested. "It really is quite lovely."

Meeghan took the catalog and handed it to her father. He looked at the dress on the page that had been dog-eared. "It's stupendous. Apparently, so is the price."

"And Meeghan's worth every penny of it," Josephine said, winking.

"That's right, Dad. Remember, I'm your only child."

"Thank God," Liam grinned. "I don't think I could take any more like you!"

"Can I order it now, even though the prom isn't until May?" Meeghan begged. "And I'll need shoes and jewelry."

"I gather nothing will do until you get your way."

"Thanks, Dad, I knew you'd come through for me," Meeghan said, planting a fleeting kiss on top of his head. "By the way, our committee is looking for parents to help serve breakfast. Can I put your names down?"

"Breakfast? Just what time does this thing end anyway?"

"Oh, come on, Dad, like you didn't stay out late on the night of your prom? So, how about it? Can I put your names down as volunteers?"

Liam exchanged a wary glance with his wife. "I'll be happy to help out, if I'm not on call that night."

"If you are, can't you switch with one of the other doctors?" She turned to Josephine. "And even if Dad can't be there, will you help out?"

Mary appeared at the doorway to say that lunch was ready. Josephine asked if they could have it served where they sat and asked Meeghan to help carry it in. When she left the room, Josephine looked gravely at her husband.

"What do you think I should tell her?"

"I think you should tell her the truth."

"Will you stay with me?" She could already feel her stomach beginning to turn over.

"If you want me to, I will."

Lunch was brought in on two trays. There were generous servings of chicken pot pie with a golden, flaky crust and a green salad with wedges of tomatoes and cucumber slices.

Josephine declined the pot pie and only picked at a small portion of salad. Although she was minus her appetite, she couldn't help but be impressed with the way Mary always managed to find the freshest produce, even in the dead of winter.

Meeghan also ate lightly, choosing instead to fill the lunch time with the planning committee's ideas for the prom. Liam, however, had worked up a hearty appetite playing in the snow and was only too willing to eat what the other two left untouched. When lunch was over, Liam told Meeghan they had something important to discuss with her and nodded to Josephine to begin.

"Meggie, I can't be counted on to help with the prom, or for your Ireland trip either." Josephine saw the question in the child's eyes and struggled to answer it honestly. "My cancer has come back."

"So? Can't the doctor give you chemotherapy again?"

"They could, but it would only put off the inevitable."

"At least you'd be alive."

"Yes, but I'd be in pain. I'd lose my hair again and my taste, and this time my hearing would be affected."

Meeghan was frightened and confused. A moment ago they had all been laughing. Why did they have to talk about sickness and ruin her good mood? "I think you just want to sabotage my prom!" she blurted. "In fact, I don't think you ever really wanted *me* at all! You only wanted Dad!"

"Meeghan!" Liam cut in. "That's nonsense, and you know it!"

Josephine held up her hand. "It's all right, Liam, she's just upset."

"No, it's true!" Meeghan insisted. "I'm only in the way around here. Like it or not, I'm always made to feel alone! You're always working, and *she*," Meeghan pointed her finger at Josephine, "is constantly sick!" Before either parent could retaliate, Meeghan had run from the room and up the stairs to her bedroom. Liam jumped up from where he sat.

Josephine put out her arm to stop him. "Leave her. She needs time to process what she's been told."

"I'll go up and talk to her."

"Just don't yell at her, please. She's entitled to her feelings."

It was a half-hour before Josephine heard him come back down again. But instead of coming into the room, he opened the hall closet and pulled his coat from the hanger. The sound was enough to alert Beau into thinking he could go with him. But when the dog scurried into the foyer, Liam gently slid him out of the way with a booted foot and slipped out the front door. He needed to be alone.

Josephine rose from her chair and walked down the hall to use the bathroom. When she came back, her stepdaughter was waiting, looking at her through red-rimmed eyes. Without saying a word Josephine opened her arms, and Meeghan fell into them. The essence of the child's health and vitality ripped at her very soul until she felt herself trembling from the power of it.

Meeghan buried her face in her stepmother's neck and wrapped her arms around her narrow hips. Against the heat of Josephine's fevered skin, she poured out her heart through tears anew. Josephine lifted the young girl's head, and the two locked eyes. A current of devotion passed between them, fusing them in a bond which they knew would withstand whatever hardship needed to be faced.

Meeghan seemed to feel the need to hang on to false hope and thus appealed one more time. "If you loved me," she said, "you would take the chemotherapy again. You'd want to live for my sake."

Josephine imagined her imminent passing from this world to the next could be no more difficult than this very moment was for her now. "And if you love me," she countered, "you will not want me to suffer."

Meeghan opened her mouth to speak, but Josephine put a finger to her lips. "If you love me, Meegie, you will let me go."

# CHAPTER *Nineteen*

Josephine slipped her bare feet into a pair of her husband's rubber galoshes and went outside to find him. The snow, which all morning had warmed beneath a radiant sun, was ideal for packing. She wished she felt well enough to stay outdoors and make a snowman.

The snow was deep against the side of the house where Liam's tracks led, but she did her best to follow in his footsteps, taking long strides while working to keep her feet inside the oversized boots.

Her hands were thrust into the pockets of her long black coat, which hung on her reduced frame like adult clothing on a small child. As she walked against the gusting wind, both ends of a long knit scarf she wore flapped in the breeze like the wings of a great red bird. She hadn't bothered to button the coat, so that her body—clad only in a pair of black stretch leggings and a gray football jersey—was exposed to the deceiving temperature.

Josephine squinted against the sun, which bounced off the crisp white snow in blinding brightness. Lifting her hand to form a visor over her brow, she looked ahead to where she saw Liam at the end of their property. He was stacking wood from a pile of logs that had been split and laid on the ground in a heap. His broad shoulders filled out the red and black checkered wool jacket as he bent to place the logs, four at a time, in his arms and slap each one with precise uniformity on top of a growing wood stack.

"So this is how you build those muscles of yours," Josephine said, sneaking up behind him.

Liam turned and dropped the wood he was holding when he saw her there, as pale as the snow in which she stood.

"Josephine! For God's sake!" He pulled off his sheepskin gloves and tossed them on top of the wood pile. "What are you doing out here dressed like that? You're going to catch your death!"

"I think it's a little too late for that, don't you?"

"*Not* funny," he scolded, pulling at her coat and fastening the top three buttons. He looked down and saw her bare ankles above the flimsy rubber boots. "Jesus! You don't have any socks on! What's the matter with you?"

"I came to see if you are all right. I was worried about you," she said, taking a tissue from her coat pocket and reaching to wipe his runny nose.

"I'm fine. There's nothing for you to worry about," he said, taking the tissue from her and shoving it in his pocket. "I just needed to clear my head and get some fresh air."

"It looks like you came to the right place," Josephine sighed, taking hold of his arm and wrapping both of hers around it. "It's beautiful out here. Look at that sky, there is not a cloud in it."

"Yeah, I see it," Liam said, propelling her around by the elbow. "Come on, I want you back in the house!"

"Wait, please," Josephine begged. "There's something I want to tell you...something that's been on my mind to say."

"You can tell me inside where it's warm."

"No. I need to say it now, right here, where no one else can overhear me."

"All right, but you'd better make it quick. I don't like your being out here." He bent to lift her off the ground. She was as light as a feather.

Josephine wound both her arms tightly around her husband's neck as he awkwardly managed to sit down on the shorter side of the wood pile with her balanced on his lap. She inhaled deeply. "Mmm, you smell so good! I love the smell of wood and fresh air!"

"Tell me quickly," Liam hurried her. "What is it you need to say?"

Josephine lovingly laid her head against his chest. The wool of his jacket scratched her softened cheek, but the solid feel of him warmed all but her ice cold feet. She nestled closer while Liam, unable to remain angry at her, lowered his chin to rest on her head.

"Meggie seemed to be better when she came back downstairs. What did you say to her?" Josephine queried.

"I can't even remember. I tried to explain what you're going through, but I only seemed to make her feel worse. I don't know how to help her through this when I feel so helpless myself."

"You're not helpless; you have been a great source of strength to *me*," Josephine praised, giving her husband a squeeze.

"Is this what you needed to tell me that couldn't be said inside the house?"

"No. I want to apologize for my behavior at the hospital a few weeks ago. I falsely accused you, and I was wrong. I know in my heart there is nothing between you and Michelle Clarkson. It was simply an overreaction on my part to Ira's bad news."

She lifted her head to look deeply into her husband's eyes. His masculine vitality was majestic; and Josephine, all too aware of her waning health, felt a cry catch in her throat before saying, "Nevertheless, Michelle's beauty threatens me."

"It shouldn't. To me, you are far more beautiful."

"A year ago, I would have believed you, but not anymore. I'm dying, and she's not. It's painful for me to think about her taking my place someday."

"Why would you think anyone ever could? Besides, it's not Michelle you should be concerned about, but Meggie. I don't know how she's going to get through this."

"She will, Liam. The child is a survivor." The cold had penetrated her clothing. She was now shivering.

"I guess I'll just have to count on Meggie to get us both through it then," Liam said, roughly rubbing his wife's arm up and down in an effort to warm her.

"You *will* be able to lean on Meggie. The amazing part is how wise she is beyond her years. It was you and Meggie long before I came into the picture. The two of you were a great team. You will be again."

"Sometimes I think we forget how to get along."

"It's like riding a bike; there are some things you just don't forget." she replied, her teeth chattering.

"That's it! You're going back inside. It wasn't good for you to be out here in the first place." Liam stood with his wife still in his arms. As he lumbered through the snow, the buckles on the rubber boots she wore jingled intermittently, keeping time with Liam's long-legged strides, while he scolded her for being the sentimental goose that she was.

Two days later, Liam held his stethoscope to his wife's chest and listened to her lungs. She had kept them both awake the night before with a rasping cough that would not abate even after she had taken a dose of prescription cough serum. With her eyes closed, Josephine lay like a rag doll in a nightgown damp with perspiration from a fever that had finally broken. Her chest heaved as she braced herself for another bout of spasmodic coughing.

Liam had Mary bring him a fresh nightgown from Josephine's dresser drawer while he slipped his wife's stick-like arms from the sleeves of her dampened gown and worked the remaining fabric over her head. While Mary helped to dress her in the clean gown, Liam called ahead to the hospital's admitting office to tell them he would be bringing his wife in for a chest x-ray when he came to do his rounds.

Down in the kitchen, Meeghan picked a rosy red apple from a bowl of fruit on the counter and hurried out. She glanced at her wrist watch, afraid she had already missed the bus. With only minutes to spare, she grabbed her coat from the closet and her school books from the table in the foyer. She hopped up two stairs to call out that she was leaving, and then marked her exit by her usual slamming of the front door. She was forced to slow down, as her boots slid on patches of ice along the long driveway. She cursed under her breath, wishing she had been permitted to drive to school.

Up ahead, Amelia waited at the bus stop. She held a stack of books in one arm while the other was frantically flailing a warning to Meeghan to hurry. The wheels of their bus came to a squeaking halt, as the chains that encased them grabbed into the ice-crusted road with a jingle resembling sleigh bells. Amelia hopped aboard and got into a seat where she waited for her friend to join her.

Meeghan boarded and breathlessly hurried down the aisle to take her customary place beside her. She fell into the leather seat with a heavy thud and immediately began an aggravated dissertation of why she was not allowed to drive to school. How degrading was it, she argued, for seniors to be seen taking the bus to school? But Amelia preferred chatting about boys, the teachers who gave too much homework, and new ways to style her hair.

Back home, Laura Bernard demanded the twins turn off the television, brush their teeth, and get ready to leave for school. It took some persuading, but eventually Scott and Jeremy Barnard did as they were told. They left with books in hand, bestowing bubblegum-flavored kisses on their mother's lips before traipsing out the front door to wait for their bus. As the O'Dells' car came down the road, the two youths waved to Liam and Josephine.

Laura was watching the boys from her window when she saw Liam's car go by. Her phone began to ring, and she waved a last goodbye to her sons before going to the kitchen to answer it. It was Mary McGlynn calling to say that Liam had just left to take Josephine to the hospital, this time for pneumonia.

# CHAPTER *Twenty*

The doctor put Josephine on antibiotics and ran a series of repetitive tests. She was released after one week and so grateful to have pulled through, she could overlook the dismal weather the month of February had brought with it. There had been no recent snowfalls, but on the roads was a filthy mixture of slush and salt that splattered vehicles and increased the sale of windshield wiper fluid at the gas stations. For Josephine, it might as well have been spring, so relieved was she to be going home.

Meeghan was at dance class when the McGlynns drove Josephine home from the hospital, and Laura and Amelia had asked to be there to welcome her back. Many friends and neighbors had sent flowers while she was convalescing, and the overpowering fragrance of them as she walked into the house reminded Josephine of the flower shop where she had spent such happy years.

Amelia waited for her mother and Mary to settle Josephine in bed before asking to see her. When she knocked and entered the room, she barely recognized the painfully thin woman smiling back at her.

"Amelia! Come in. Come in, dear," Josephine urged. The pain medication they had given her in the hospital made her drowsy, but she was fairly comfortable and up to the visit, despite her fatigue.

"Hi, Mrs. O'Dell, I hope I'm not bothering you. I came to see how you're feeling."

"I'm better, thank you, Amelia. How about you? Are you enjoying school? Are you doing well with your riding?"

"Everything's fine, thanks." She looked toward her mother, who in turn merely nodded for her to proceed with what she had come to do.

Reaching into a small gift bag she had brought with her Amelia said, "Now it's my turn now to bring you a gift, but you've got to close your eyes."

Josephine lowered her head into her hands. Only Laura, standing behind her, could see the vertebrae jutting out from under her friend's translucent skin; the fingers of her hands seemed as thin as a chicken's claw.

"Okay, you can open your eyes now," Amelia said. She had lifted a blue ribbon from the bag and was holding it up with pride.

"Well, will you look at that," Josephine exclaimed, reaching out to inspect the prestigious award.

"I won it for Dressage."

"I've got to admit, Amelia was truly outstanding at the competition," Laura boasted. "You were right, Josie, to help convince me to let her ride again. She definitely has a gift for the sport."

"She obviously does," Josephine agreed, holding the ribbon out for Amelia. "Thank you for showing me your winnings."

"No, no, it's for you," Amelia insisted.

"For me? But, I can't accept it. This ribbon is yours—it belongs with all the others you've won."

"Please, Mrs. O'Dell, I want you to keep it. I won it because of you. I wouldn't be riding again if it hadn't been for you believing in me."

"Well then, thank you, Amelia. I shall treasure it. Laura, would you do me the honor of hanging this beautiful award on my bedpost for me?" When it had been done, Josephine turned, straining to admire it. "Ah, now that's nice! Thank you."

But the exertion proved to be too much, and she coughed and fell back on the pillows. Amelia's eyes were wide with fright.

"Sweetheart," her mother said, "why don't you wait for me downstairs, okay? I want to help make Josie comfortable and then we'll go home."

The young girl needed no persuasion. Looking at the sick woman made her uneasy, even though Josephine's coughing had abated. Relieved to be excused, Amelia said, "It was nice to see you, Mrs. O'Dell. I hope you feel better."

"I am honored you gave me your winning ribbon, Amelia."

"You helped me win it; I thought you should have it."

When they were alone, Laura sat on the edge of the bed and lifted Josephine's hand. She held it between her own two, the cool arid feel of the skin a subtle reminder that her friend's life was ebbing away. Laura held her hand and listened to her shallow breathing. "Josie? Honey, can I do anything for you? Are you all right?"

"I'm just tired, that's all."

"Are you in pain?"

"Always."

"Oh, Sweetie, tell me what I can do for you."

Josephine had closed her eyes again. For a moment she did not answer. Then she gave Laura's hand a squeeze. "Watch over Meggie for me, Laura. I don't want to leave her; God knows the thought of it is killing me faster than the cancer is." She let out a series of hacking coughs, and her face wrinkled in pain.

Laura poured water from a pitcher on the bed stand into a small glass. She handed it to Josephine, who took a few sips before continuing. "Liam tries, but he's never known how to really talk to Meeghan. These are important years for her. She's going to need me, and I won't be here for her." Tears appeared in the corners of her eyes. "Will you do that for me? Will you watch over Meeghan?"

"Sweetheart," Laura said, lifting Josephine's fragile hand to her lips and kissing it, "you know that I will."

Knowing a Hospice nurse had begun coming to the house daily was not what told Josephine she was nearing the end. She already knew it. She could feel it. Just looking at her reflection each time she passed a mirror confirmed it.

Liam suggested that, depending on how she was feeling, she might enjoy seeing her sister and Robert and the Silvermans. Ned and Matthew had sent a postcard from their sight-seeing tour of Italy saying they would visit when they returned. But Liam feared that by the time they came home, it would be too late.

Marsha and Marc came to stay at County Glen for three days, doing what they could to help with Josephine's homecare. Marc busied himself by lending a hand to Patrick while Liam was at work, or exercising Beau on long walks and thereby escaping the gloominess in the house.

Marsha, on the other hand, was reluctant to leave Josephine's bedside. She bustled in and out of the rooms—picking up, and putting down; asking questions of, and making demands on, an irritable Mary. Her well-meaning was quickly growing on the housekeeper's nerves, who only wished she could exert her Irish temper and send the woman packing, thereby leaving Josephine's care in her own capable hands.

On the day they finally were to go back to Clapton, Marsha broke down. She became so distraught and inconsolable at having to say goodbye that Liam insisted on giving her a sedative. Within half an hour she was drowsy enough to leave without making a scene, though her eyes were swollen and her heart heavy and filled with despair.

At the end of the same week, Alex and Robert arrived from Cape Cod. They had left their son with Robert's mother so he wouldn't miss school. Alex brought enough clothes with her to stay as long as was needed. In her suitcase she included her black wool dress, which she despised packing, for doing so made her feel she was sealing her sister's fate.

Due to a scheduled run with his boat, Robert could only stay one night. He said his goodbyes to his sister-in-law, promising to bring young Robby to visit his aunt when she felt up to it. As soon as he had gone, Liam mandated no other visitors be permitted into the house, not even Laura Barnard.

He had Mary see to it that all phone calls were channeled into their answering machine and that the ringers on all phones be turned off. His office and the hospital were to reach him by means of his pager or cell phone. His practiced eye knew the time was near.

ɞ

Josephine O'Dell lay in her large four poster bed in a drug-induced state as her life ebbed away. She lay in the only position which allowed her any comfort: on her back with her legs straight and her arms close to her sides.

Sundae sat sphinx-like near the foot of the bed. The cat's own body had been diminished to half its size with age and grieving; her lusterless calico coat was thin and balding. For nearly twenty years the two had been inseparable, so much so that even now they appeared to have taken on an uncanny likeness to one another.

Josephine slowly opened her eyes. She listened to the beating of cold rain as it slapped against the bedroom windows. March had indeed come in like a lion; but despite the dreary time of year, the sound of rain was soothing. As long as Hospice kept her medicated, she was comfortable.

Although she was confined to bed, she could easily visualize the bleak scene outside. She closed her eyes and imagined tiny crocus bulbs pushing upwards to break through the earth beside their stronger daffodil siblings. The front flower beds, matted now from the last three months of snowfall, would be drooped with soggy pods and dried brown stalks, a sad promise of colors and fragrances to come.

"Josie, can you open your eyes? Guess who's here?" a gentle voice careened.

Summoned from her reverie, Josephine's eyelids fluttered several times before opening to hooded half-moons.

"That's my girl." Rosalie, the nurse assigned by Hospice, continued to urge her patient.

The increasingly frequent doses of morphine blurred Josephine's senses, so that when she did as she was instructed, her eyes were drawn to Rosalie's blouse with its whimsical teddy bear print. Although it was juvenile for a woman of Rosalie's age, the teddy bear design suited her personality. Just like a teddy bear, Rosalie was soft and embraceable. An upsweep of light brown hair framed a face of compassionate expression, while her heart held stories of patients she had helped along their final journey.

Rosalie's soothing hand, warm and tender, lay feather-light on the bony veined one beneath it. "It's your daughter. She's come to cheer you on this rainy day." She gingerly enveloped Josephine in her arms, and with what seemed like a hundred hands, pulled her gently forward. Josephine braced herself for the pain that was sure to accompany the simple maneuver, but Meeghan was worth the pain.

A striking young woman in a pale blue sweat suit stepped cautiously into the room. She possessed a smile so genuinely dazzling, it seemed to have entered the room before her.

"Hello, Josie, I've brought you some early spring," Meeghan said, holding an umbrella explosion of colored tulips in both hands as if it were a wedding bouquet.

"Come. Sit." A birdlike hand, loosely encased in the roomy sleeve of a white linen nightgown, weakly patted the covers. "You're my sunshine on...this rainy day, you know. Wherever did you... find tulips this early?"

Meeghan pulled a nearby rocking chair beside the bed and sat down. "Dante brought me to a florist in Manhattan when he picked me up from dance class." These words were spoken like a prayer. They floated in the air—a whisper of a sweet, minted breath. "He sends his love and wants to know when he can come to visit you." Her uplifted tone could not fool Josephine, who clearly recognized it as an attempt to suppress an underlying fear.

Rosalie carefully arranged several fluffy pillows behind her patient's back to secure her comfort and then, offering to put the tulips in a vase, silently left the two women to their visit.

"Pull the chair...closer," Josephine instructed. "Let me look at you."

Meeghan did as she was asked, folding her hands, with their long tapered fingers and short clean nails, softly in her lap.

*She is incredibly beautiful! Born to be the dancer she's become.* Josephine filled her senses with the vision of the woman-child. It revitalized her just to look into the lively green eyes, an exact rendition of Liam's, gently smiling back at her.

Meeghan's thick, shiny brown hair was pulled back with a headband to expose a perfectly rounded forehead. Her creamy complexion, with its faint sprinkling of cinnamon-colored freckles, was set off by the baby blue sweat suit she wore. She cocked her head to one side; and in the silence that followed, young eyes met old. What she saw made her heart lurch.

Her stepmother's cancer had made a rapid advance. A once robust woman, full of life and laughter and with a lion's mane of golden hair, Josephine was now reduced to a skeletal eighty pounds. Angular bones jutted from her neck and shoulders while her legs looked as if two broomsticks were laid side by side beneath the bedding.

Her generous mouth, donor of a million kisses, winced periodically in grimaces of pain, causing the lips to fold into a single thin line. Seconds later they would reopen, flushed with fever, their corners weakly turned upward in false bravado.

Meeghan longed to see a sign of vitality and found it in her stepmother's eyes. They remained unchanged and lovingly familiar. Soft brown and deeply lidded, they were alive with hundreds of untold stories. Meeghan caught the flickering of something deep and unidentifiable in them...could it be regret? Whatever it was she thought she had seen there left her feeling haunted and alone.

Within silent seconds, a physical and emotional inventory had been taken by both women and assessed in their hearts. All that remained now was to make the most of what little time they had left together.

Ever so gently, Meeghan lifted her stepmother's hand and placed it in her own. She would do her best to keep the pain of emotion from reflecting in her voice, and she was willing to stay there, holding her stepmother's hand, for as long as she was needed.

"You will be pleased to know," she told her, "that Dante has been approached by a New York architectural firm, regarding a position..."

## CHAPTER *Twenty-One*

Josephine chose this time alone with Meeghan to present her with her surprise gift. She instructed her to bring it out from inside the closet where she had kept it hidden. It was a large box, with top and bottom handsomely wrapped in blue gingham fabric and tied with bright green satin ribbon.

Meeghan untied the bow and gently lifted the lid. She removed a weighty fabric neatly wrapped in a scented tissue and laid it across her lap. Carefully she opened the folds of tissue paper and gasped. Softly folded was a hand-crafted quilt cut from squares of fabrics of the past. Each square had been lovingly donated by Josephine, Alex, Marsha, Laura, and Amelia. Each had been cut from an assortment of fabrics sentimentally meaningful. The squares had then been placed in a traditional patchwork pattern and sewn together to form the finished quilt that Meeghan now held against her heart.

She recognized swatches from favorite pieces of clothing and linens: from curtains which hung in her room when she was a child, to Amelia's childhood riding jacket; a swatch of chintz from Marsha's flower shop, and a square of Josephine's wedding dress. There was even a square cut from Liam's lab coat, complete with a pocket monogrammed *Liam O'Dell, MD.*

"This is unbelievable!" Meeghan cried, pressing the quilt to her cheek. "It's extraordinary!"

"Glad you like it...," Josephine whispered. "It was sewn with love."

"It's totally out of this world, and I will treasure it always!"

Meeghan carefully refolded the quilt and laid it beside her and removed the next gift from the box. This one was a scrapbook filled with the four women's all-time greatest recipes. With each one the donor had included a write-up of where the recipe originated and why it was a favorite. One of them was Marsha's chicken recipe, marked as the dish she served the night Josephine met Liam.

The next gift opened was a leather journal. Josephine had begun writing in it after her first marriage failed and had continued keeping a periodic account of her life through the years.

"All my secrets...," she said. "Don't tell..."

"I won't, you can trust me." As Meeghan fanned through the pages, reading clips and passages, her lower lip began to tremble. The written words blurred with tears, which hung like jewels on her lower lids.

"Come now," Josephine soothed, "Don't cry."

Meeghan wiped her eyes and blew her nose. Then she lifted the last gift out of the box. This one was the heaviest, and she tried to guess what it was. When she uncovered Josephine's jewelry box under the wrapping, Meeghan was aghast.

"Oh, Josie, you can't give me your jewelry!"

"I can...and did."

"What about Alex, and Marsha?"

"Done. The rest...is yours."

Reverently, Meeghan lifted the lid of the ornate mahogany box. There were two diamond rings and two wedding bands, gold and silver bracelets, earrings, a strand of pearls, and the small gold oval pin belonging to her grandmother that Josephine had worn on her wedding day. All of it gleamed like a pirate's treasure upon black velvet lining.

Meeghan reached down and removed the two wedding bands. The gold one had been given to Josephine by Anthony; the platinum band, from Liam. Both had once been given in love, but only one with everlasting intention.

"These are so beautiful!" Meeghan slipped the two bands on the ring finger of her right hand. Once again her eyes filled with tears, and her voice broke. "Oh, Josie, what can I say?" Closing the jewelry box and laying it aside, Meeghan covered her face with her hands and gave in to her emotion.

"That you will...miss me," Josephine sighed, closing her eyes against her own emotion, which ripped open her heart until she could barely breathe.

☙

Josephine died on April tenth, just two days before her fiftieth birthday. A black silk ribbon wreath hung outside the house, its somber shade a tragic message against the stark whiteness of a welcoming door. Fastened to the wreath, Amelia's blue ribbon hung on the side of it like a blue angel floating on the black arm of death.

Neighbors sent notes, flowers and food while suffering the news of her passing. Many of them had, only months before, offered up futile prayers asking God to perform a miracle, but their prayers had gone unanswered.

Liam appeared to have aged overnight. There were dark circles under his eyes, and the skin on his face and neck seemed to sag beneath the weight of his own grief. He stood in the dining room with a cup of coffee in his hand and Patrick McGlynn's bony arm around his shoulders while Mary McGlynn, dressed in black, robotically went about the room setting the serving station with pastries and fruit. Intermittently the family came together in the dining room, gently embracing one another before quietly helping themselves to steaming cups of her strong coffee.

The sun quickly climbed in the cloudless sky, casting its warm morning rays across a lawn that had finally begun turning green after a long season's thaw. Liam frowned as he witnessed a pair of squirrels performing a bizarre mating dance while they scampered over and about the stone wall beside the aging oak tree. Like the sunshine, the squirrels' carefree abandon mocked him in his devastation.

Meeghan entered the room, looking especially lost and bereft. She wore a short black dress, black stockings, and a pair of black stacked heels. Around her neck hung Josephine's strand of shell-pink pearls, which seemed to make a dramatic statement of their own.

Liam's heart swelled as he looked at his daughter. Together they had stayed awake on the night Josephine died, both of them holding her hands as her erratic breathing faded into the finality of nothingness. That night Meeghan had turned from a child of advantage to a woman of endurance, and Liam could not have been more proud of her.

Alex came to quietly stand by Meeghan's side, offering unspoken comfort by slipping her arm around her niece's waist. It left Robert standing alone, looking oddly out of place and fidgeting uncomfortably in his suit and tie. His large hands hung helplessly at his sides while he looked to see how he could make himself useful. Eventually Patrick McGlynn asked his assistance in bringing the cars around to the front of the house. It was time to leave for the funeral home.

As the two-car procession pulled out of the driveway and down the road, Meeghan looked out her window at the house next door. There she saw David Barnard, dressed in a dark suit, trying his best to round up Beau and Huckleberry and bring them indoors before he and Laura left for the service. Amelia, along with Dante and Bruce, would already be at the funeral home waiting. Their friendship was Meeghan's only comforting thought.

Sundae lay like a flimsy rag on the windowsill of the master bedroom, watching the family take their leave. Alone in the room, the animal's grief knew no bounds. She opened wide her tiny, nearly toothless mouth and emitted a series of cries so mournful as to be frightening. Instinctively she knew her own time was coming, that her job here was done. Without her beloved mistress, she had no purpose.

The family gathered first at the funeral home for an intimate prayer service and for a last viewing before the casket was closed and transported to the little church where Liam and his wife had exchanged wedding vows less than two years before.

The congregation who came to honor her memory filled the pews and lined the side isles in a final show of respect. There was not a person present whose life Josephine had not touched in some way. From the garden club ladies to the church guild; from the faculty at Meeghan's school to the doctors and their wives, they gathered in solemn prayer to bid her soul farewell. The air inside the little church was filled with the spice-scented haze of incense, as the priest now sent Josephine Mitchell O'Dell on a prayerful journey home.

The sun was setting by the time the last house guests took their leave. It had been arranged that Alexandra and Robert and the Silvermans would stay. Knowing sleep would not be coming easily that night, they sat by the fire with Liam, drinking wine and reminiscing about Josephine and the times shared together.

Emotionally exhausted as they were, they put off going to bed. They knew that waking up the next day meant that they would have to continue their lives without Josephine. She had fought the fight and lost; and now each of them had, in turn, lost her.

Upstairs, Meeghan stood naked in front of her bedroom mirror except for the strand of pink pearls she had worn to the funeral. Each lustrous bead was the size of a pea, the center one resting below the soft hollow in her throat. In the illumination of soft lamplight, they blended with the lucent paleness of her skin, like dew on a rose petal.

Reaching behind her neck, she unfastened the gold clasp and enfolded the slippery strand in the palm of her hand. The pearls were warm and, raising them to her nostrils, she inhaled the familiar scent of Chanel No.5. She pressed them to her cheek, rolling their iridescent smoothness against her skin while she closed her eyes and remembered Josephine.

# CHAPTER *Twenty-Two*

It had been an incredible two weeks shared in Dublin with her dance troupe. On unfamiliar soil they had blended together and worked as a family unit, studying the heritage of Celtic dance and visiting those places where, generations before them, many of their ancestors had been born.

Meeghan thought about her father, alone in New York, and visualized him pining for her. She suddenly wished she was home, rather than in Ireland—in an abyss of uncertainty—waiting to meet the birthmother she had never known. They were to meet inside Kildare Cathedral, a restored thirteenth-century structure, in the last pew on the left, at the appointed hour of four o'clock. Meeghan had purposely arrived early.

The cathedral was a place of interest both historically and religiously, having started out centuries before as a small church built near a great oak tree where the eponymous Saint Brigid founded a religious settlement in the fifth century. Had she not been so nervous, she could have enjoyed the church's many points of interest, including its font—the design of which used the symbolism of the story of the patron saint—or the outside remains of the ancient High Cross of Kildare. Instead she sat trembling, holed up on a seasonal August afternoon in the back of a cathedral, in the last pew on the left.

The sun, streaming through an enormous stained-glass window overhead, cast her khaki skirt and white blouse in psychedelic colors and made her tanned complexion appear golden. Without having ever met her, there was no way Meeghan could have known how strongly her features resembled those of her mother. Liam was the only person who could have attested to his daughter's uncanny resemblance to Shannon Flaherty.

Reaching into her backpack, she pulled out an ivory envelope, slightly creased and bent at one corner. Her name had been attractively penned across the front in Josephine's handsome handwriting and was dated three weeks before she died. Meeghan held it in her hands as tenderly as she would have a bird with a broken wing, running her thumb across the penmanship before turning the envelope over, lifting its flap, and removing the single-folded page.

Although every word was etched in her mind so that she could have recited the letter verbatim, she never tired of reading it.

*Dear Meeghan,*

*For so long, I believed I would never know the joy of having had a child of my own—and then came you. You have been a treasure, Meggie, bringing me more happiness in two years than I experienced in a lifetime.*

*I love being here for you, just as I love your being here for me, too. Hearing about your everyday happenings feels as if you are handing me a potion from the fountain of youth—your stories make me feel young (and healthy) again. Likewise, sharing my experiences with you joins our spirits closer and makes me hope that I am perhaps passing to you valuable advice which may help you later in life.*

*Don't be afraid to do what we talked about. Locating your mother while in Ireland, despite your father's objections, is a worthwhile goal. She may be regretting the decision she made eighteen years ago. If so, she will need your forgiveness.*

*Should you find your mother unreceptive, forgive her still, for she may not be capable of recognizing an earth-angel.*

*Remember to love your father and forgive him his faults, too, just as he always forgave us ours. He is a good man and deserves your respect.*

*Lastly, I want you to know this: I could not have loved you more had you passed through my own body. You are, and always will be, my Meeghan, captain of her own ship.*

*Set sail, sweetheart, in search of your destiny. Never be afraid, for I am with you—always.*

*My love is eternal,*
*Josephine*

Meeghan refolded the letter and tucked it away. She glanced at her watch, wondering if she had been stood up. As she looked into the face of every tourist who walked by, she hoped one of them would be *the one*. It embarrassed her to think her mother would be late for such a monumentally important meeting. Behind her, she heard her name called by a woman with a strong Irish accent—a woman who instinctively knew who she was.

"Meeg-han."

"Yes. Hello." Meeghan quaked with apprehension. She stepped out in to the aisle and stood face-to-face with a woman who looked like an older version of herself.

At thirty-seven, Shannon Flaherty O'Connor was still a beautiful woman, with a flawless complexion that defied her age, but with the pallor of one unaccustomed to being in the sun.

She appeared rigid, moving forward as though she were molded from a single block of wood that could glide along the floor on wheels.

Her arms hung straight down at her sides until she extended one from the shoulder joint. "I am Shannon O'Connor," she said, barely shaking Meeghan's hand. "I fear this is uncomfortable for us both."

"If you like, we could talk outside," Meeghan offered.

"This will be fine right here. This cathedral is ancient; there is history all around us. We can sit for a few minutes, but I can't stay long."

Shannon turned to enter the pew and Meeghan followed timidly. She noticed that her mother's lusterless hair was worn in a severely tight knot at the nape of her neck, a fitting style for the drab suit and matronly shoes she wore. Yet an undeniable trace of hidden beauty was visible beneath a face void of emotion; and the two lips, which were momentarily pulled tightly into a single line, otherwise appeared soft and supple. She could be pretty if she smiled, Meeghan thought.

They sat to face one another in the pew, away from the small groups of parishioners and sightseeing tourist who wondered the perimeter with flash cameras. Shannon's clothing emitted an earthy, country scent—like fresh hay—which Meeghan found undeniably comforting.

"Where are you staying while you are here?" Shannon inquired.

"In Drogehda, with some friends of ours." Liam had forewarned her not to divulge too much personal information.

"How long do you plan to stay?"

"I only have until the end of the week. I thought while I'm here, perhaps we could spend one of those days together...if you have the time, that is."

"I'm afraid that won't be possible."

"Why? I was hoping—"

"Meeg-han, there is something you need to understand. I have a husband and a family. They don't know anything about you. Also, I have my job. I'm a college professor with a very busy schedule."

Meeghan's heart began to pound. She hadn't come this far to get dismissed so easily. "So basically, what you're saying is that you have no desire to get to know me, right? That you're not at all sorry for leaving my dad and me all those years ago, right?" She was trying not to raise her voice.

"Please do not speak to me in that tone." Shannon peered over her shoulder to see if anyone had overheard them. "Perhaps this was not a good idea after all." She rose from where she was sitting, gaining height as she stiffened.

"I can't believe this!" Meeghan whispered, no longer concerned about making a good first impression. "I thought you just might be happy to see me, that you would want to get to know me! How stupid was I?"

"Don't you see, Meeg-han? You only thought about yourself. You never gave a thought to the life I've made for myself and the effect your coming here could have on me and my family."

Shannon walked out the other end of the pew, hastily heading for the back of the church. She pushed open the heavy wooden doors and stepped out into the glaring sunlight.

"Wait!" Meeghan called after her. She followed her mother outside. "Is this how you are going to leave me? Was my coming here nothing more than an inconvenience to you?"

Shannon looked at the young woman standing beside her. But instead of seeing a daughter, she saw a pathetic-looking stranger, one that she had never come to know.

"What is it you want from me, Meeg-han?" she implored.

"I want to *know* you." Meeghan's eyes filled with tears. "I want my mother!"

For a moment there was silence. But when she spoke, Shannon's staunch presence was as void of emotion as the rock she was standing on. "I am sorry you traveled all this way, then," she declared, "for I fear you may have wasted your time."

# CHAPTER Twenty-Three

The evening was alive with the sounds of summertime. Locusts' soft humming grew to a fevered pitch within seconds. Frogs croaked their throaty duets from the wetland where the wild roses grew, while tiny fireflies lit the yard, edible targets to the nocturnal bat in search of a meal.

Meeghan and Dante reveled in it all, only letting go of each other's hand long enough to slap at an occasional mosquito, as they made their way down the long stone driveway. The weeks they were separated while Meeghan was in Ireland seemed a lifetime of absence for both of them.

Ignoring the rules of etiquette, they had slipped away from the small dinner party being held in honor of her return. A few itchy bites on their arms and legs were a small price to pay for the chance to be alone together.

Dante pulled Meeghan to him, bringing her closer so he could plant a tender kiss on her sweet mouth.

She looked at him and smiled. "Thanks, I needed that."

"I'm only too happy to oblige," he grinned, squeezing her close to his side. "So, you told me all about the tour with your troupe, but you're not saying much about your mother, except that she didn't exactly welcome you with open arms."

"No, she didn't," Meeghan said. "But, you know something? In the end, I got the feeling she was pleased I had gone to the trouble of finding her."

"What makes you say that?"

"I'm not sure. I mean, she started out totally hardened when she first met me, but eventually she began to soften. It turned out we saw each other three times that week, and each time our visits were longer and longer. In the end, I could tell she really wanted to get to know me. She even asked about my major and was interested to know which college I chose."

"What did she say?"

"She had heard of Wellesley, and she thinks Women's Studies an appropriate major for our times."

"Did you tell her about me?"

"Of course I did, silly." Meeghan giggled. "Actually, Shannon wanted to know all about you."

"You call her by her first name? Doesn't that feel kind of weird?"

"It does, but our relationship is way too new to call her anything more endearing."

"You mean, like *mom*?"

"Exactly."

It was getting dark, and the mosquitoes were gaining in number. Meeghan and Dante turned to head back toward the house with only a sliver of pale moon to light their way.

They walked a short distance in silence before Dante asked, "So, did you tell her that we're going to get married after college?"

"We are?"

"That's my plan. I've already got the drawings started for the design of the house we're going to build."

"Oh, I see," Meeghan laughed. "And tell me, mister architect, will I have any say in these future plans of yours?"

"You'll have the burden of convincing your mother to be here for it." Dante grew serious. "I wonder if she and your stepfather would actually come over from Ireland to attend?"

Meeghan laughed again and held up an open palm. "Whoa, baby! You're going way too fast for me! Let's just deal with my next four years of college for now, all right? Shannon and I have a lifetime of catching up to do. We need to have a relationship between us before I can discuss yours and mine with her."

"Do you think you two will ever get to that point?"

"I'm not sure, but I hope so. Josie's letter said I should learn to forgive my mother for deserting me, whether she regrets what she did or not."

Dante softly cupped her chin in his hand. "You have a lot to forgive her for."

"I believe I've already begun. Josie made it possible by what she taught me about *destiny* and 'sailing my own ship.' It's like that hourglass she gave me when we first met. I know now that I have a lot to do with my life, and I need to try to do it all before the sand runs out."

"Ships? Hourglasses? Meggie, what are you talking about?"

"I'm talking about being the captain of my own ship."

Dante was trying to comprehend what she was saying. "So, then if you're the captain, who am I?"

"Why, you're my First Mate!"

For the second time that evening, Dante pulled Meeghan's body close and kissed her. They held on tight, smiling into each other's eyes and feeling for the moment that everything was right in their world.

Quietly they slipped back in the house by way of the kitchen entry and were there but seconds when they heard Ira Goldstein's wife make comment.

"I must say, Liam, I've never seen your daughter looking more beautiful. However did you do it?"

"Do what?"

"Turn out such a stunning young lady?"

"I'm afraid I can't take any credit there," Liam said. "It was Josephine who took the duckling and turned her into a swan."

As if on cue, Meeghan entered the room holding Dante's hand. Her face still held the blush of romance; her gracefulness, as she mingled among the guests, could only be compared to poetry in motion.

There appeared to be an energy surrounding her—an aura, so to speak, which cast its vibrant, magnetic spell on every person with whom she spoke.

Only the cat, feeble and arthritically crippled, was aware of the power in the room below. Only Sundae, crouched at the top of the stairway, recognized the tangible presence that moved silently and invisibly among the guests.

ଓ

"Grandma says she likes her eggs scrambled, so first we add some milk...like this. And we stir them...like this." Dante poured a small amount of milk from the container into the four raw eggs in the bowl. Taking his daughter's hand in his, he demonstrated how to whisk the mixture until it was a frothy consistency.

"Then what do we do, Daddy?"

"Then we get you down off this stool," he said, helping his four year old daughter to hop to her feet. "And then I pour these eggs into the frying pan, like this."

"Can I see?" A chubby hand clutched at his pajama pants.

"No, no, Josie," he replied, "the stove is very hot. "Why don't you go tell Gramma that breakfast is almost ready?"

When she had gone, Dante removed the bacon from the oven, poured two cups of coffee and placed them on the table opposite a pink plastic cup filled with orange juice. His mother-in-law entered the kitchen, holding her granddaughter's hand.

"Ah, you spoil me! I had all good intentions of being the one to cook breakfast this morning." In bathrobe and slippers, Shannon O'Connor shuffled to the table.

"No problem. I had a lot of help," Dante said, winking at his little girl. Clearing his throat, he added, "I want to thank you, Shannon, for coming. We appreciate it, and I know it means the world to Meggie to have you near."

"Why wouldn't I come? I came when Josephine was born; I'm here for my grandson, too," Shannon retorted, displaying the occasional rigidity her daughter and son-in-law had come to recognize as a classic trait of hers. She softened her tone by changing the subject. "Dante, I cannot help but adore this house! Meeg-han must be so proud of you for designing it. Speaking of my daughter, has she called yet?"

"No, but I suspect we'll be hearing from her any time now. She'll be excited about coming home today."

"And she's bringing my new baby brother!" Josie cried. She had been coloring a picture, which she now pushed aside.

"Yes," her father replied, "Mommy will be coming home with Glen Thomas. Now eat the rest of the eggs we made, otherwise you won't be strong enough to hold him." Dante filled her miniature fork with a few pieces of the fluffy yellow eggs and propelled it into the small *o* his daughter formed with her mouth.

"Gramma, will you...tell me that...story?" Josie asked through a mouth full of partially-chewed egg.

"Swallow before you speak," her father instructed.

"Which story, Josephine?" Shannon asked. "Do you mean the one about when I flew on the plane from Ireland to come to see you when you were born?"

A cap of shiny brunette curls bobbed up and down while two lively green eyes danced with the anticipation of a story she already knew by heart.

The phone rang as Dante was carrying the dishes to the sink. "I'll bet that's Meeghan. Will you answer it, Mom?"

Shannon reached for the receiver. "Hello? Why, hello, dear; we've been waiting for your call. How did you sleep? Did my new grandson do a lot of fussing...?"

"Can I talk to her?" Josie interrupted. "I want to talk to Mommy!"

"Just a minute," Dante corrected. "You must wait your turn."

"We're fine, just fine," Shannon was saying. "Your husband made me eggs and bacon for breakfast..."

"Me, too, Gramma! I cooked the eggs, too!"

"Hold on, Meeg-han. Someone is anxious to talk to her mommy," Shannon handed the cordless phone to her granddaughter.

Minutes later, the child said, "Daddy, Mommy wants to talk to you." She handed her father the phone and came to stand by her grandmother's side. "Gramma, do you know how long it is till an hour?"

"Yes, I do. Why?"

"Because Mommy said we can go get her from the hospital in an hour. Do you know what an hour *looks* like?"

"What it *looks* like?" her grandmother asked. "Well, no, I cannot say that I do."

"I can show you!" She skipped out of the room, returning a minute later holding an ornate wooden hourglass with both hands. "This is what an hour looks like!"

Fearing an accident, Shannon helped stand the hourglass on the table and watched as her granddaughter carefully turned it upside down. Immediately the sand began to sift, in a single thin thread, from the top globe into the bottom one.

Dante finished his phone conversation and placed the receiver in its cradle. He spotted the hourglass and frowned. "Josephine, what are you doing with that? You know it belongs to Mommy."

"I know, Daddy! I am showing it to Grandma."

"It's lovely," Shannon commented. "Where did it come from?"

"Grandma Josephine gave it to Mommy when she was a girl," the child explained.

"Well, it's very nice, indeed," Shannon commented. "But if your mother is expecting us at the hospital in an hour, we had better hurry and get dressed."

"Come on, little girl," Dante said, scooping his daughter into his arms and tossing her gently in the air. "Let's go get ready!"

"Wait! Daddy, wait!" Josie cried. "First I have to tell Grandma about the sand...and the dreams..."

"No time, Pumpkin; Mommy's waiting."

"But I need to tell Grandma about doing what you want to do before the sand runs out!"

"Whatever is she talking about?" Shannon asked, taking hold of the squirming child to quiet her.

Dante shook his head and let out a sigh of fatigue. "It's a long story," he said, rolling his eyes to heaven, "and Josie here can tell you the whole thing in its entirety."

"Well that's just fine, because Grandma has all the time in the world, doesn't she, sweetheart?" Shannon cooed, kissing her granddaughter soundly on a plump cheek, as she held her hand and headed down the hall.